Cobblestone Dreams

by

Brent Bender

authorHOUSE™

1663 LIBERTY DRIVE, SUITE 200
BLOOMINGTON, INDIANA 47403
(800) 839-8640
WWW.AUTHORHOUSE.COM

First published by AuthorHouse 12/09/05

ISBN: 1-4184-9488-7 (e)
ISBN: 1-4184-9487-9 (sc)

Library of Congress Control Number: 2004096439

Printed in the United States of America
Bloomington, Indiana

This book is printed on acid-free paper.

Cover art by Doug Berry
Editing: Stephen Frothingham

Table of Contents

I — Discern Desire

"Andy, that was amazing!"

Tony Stewart seemed more hyped than usual, which is amazing for a man who drinks more coffee than water. To me, it wasn't amazing; it was one place too little. I longed for a top-three placing at USCF collegiate championships, but to come that close, I might as well come in dead last. Tony patted me on the back, handed me a cold bottle of water and a washcloth, and began to address me and the rest of the Appalachian State University cycling team.

"Now I know you guys are happy with this result, but we really could have pulled off something much better! Andy Bennet, Andy Bennet— when will you learn that racing isn't about who is strongest, but who is the smartest with the strengths they've got? I saw you covering way too many attacks at the start. If you had waited, you would have made the winning break and possibly given the rest of your teammates a better placing."

He was right; application of gray matter didn't happen quite like I had wanted. I started the race and wanted to prove my place, flaunt my power, and ride like a king. Instead, I watched the winning break roll away and I was helpless to stop it. Still, I gutted it out to make a go of it to the end and slipped away from the group to solo in for fourth place. This result, plus the criterium and team time trial, and the ASU cycling team came out with a second-place overall in the Division I conference. Not too bad at all.

I looked at my transparent reflection, my forehead pressed against the glass, as the blurred vision of the endless landscape lulled me. I always enjoyed the travel; it was my time to think and reflect.

Twenty-one years of existence, two years of college, and six years of cycling. I had no idea where my life was going, but I felt a hunger inside. I tried to place what it was exactly and it hit me … the bike. At the ripe young age of fifteen, I happened upon a special place, the Lehigh Valley Velodrome. My best friend Alex Gardner wanted to see his brother Tyler race at the velodrome during the premier Friday night racing. It was there I was hooked, secured by an unknown force whose grip was as real as steel. I watched as riders literally flew mere inches from me, pushing the air so hard my hair brushed my face as I stood against the track wall. The lights, the crowd, the speed, the tactics … I was amazed, truly stupefied. There seemed no real logic to it all. Only one winner out of fifty riders! Then there were the blazing speeds, one gear, and no brakes! How was this possible? One doesn't just go that fast, bumping that many riders, have no brakes, and be a normal person. I was right about one thing.

I stood wide eyed all night, trying not to even blink so I wouldn't miss a revolution of a solitary pedal stroke. My hands were so sore from banging on the bleachers that I had blisters the next morning. I knew then I had found something special and signed up for the track's development program the very next day. It was the start of something great.

My bike and I were inseparable. On Friday nights when other kids were out with friends at the local football game, I was racing track or driving to a race for the weekend. Most of my friends just thought of it as "that sport where you shave your legs," or "Oh, you do BMX, cool." I remember a pretty young girl I met at the mall one night. She giggled and smiled; the talk was good.

Then she asked, "So what do you like to do?"

Eagerly I replied, "Oh, I race bikes, it's so much fun! I love it!"

I saw her eyes widen in interest as she leaned forward with sparkling eyes and voluptuous lips.

"Oh, I love bikes! The speeds they go are amazing! Guys look so sexy on motorcycles!"

Click, click, went my brain and I uttered hesitantly.

"Oh, that's not what I do. I race bicycles."

That pretty much killed the interest right there. I didn't care; it was my passion.

From the track I started to race on the road, and then later picked up cyclocross and mountain biking to break up the harsh northeast winters. I enjoyed those days with relentless lust, just me and my bike, riding open roads. It was my freedom, my escape and I loved it.

The years went by quickly and there was much success and failure. I found myself in great form the years I had the will to actually apply myself. There wasn't much pressure from my parents to do cycling or to succeed at it. I was left to my own accord and pursuits, so all my motivation came from within. Seven years later, almost every one of my friends I started racing with stopped riding or even quit cycling. I watched as they developed a bitter taste for a sport that had once brought them so much love.

I never put much thought into doing other things with my time. The bike gave me everything I wanted from life, but recently I had been feeling conflicted and utterly confused. I felt this hunger inside me; it was being fed, but it wanted more.

I watched the sun slowly faded into flickers of crimson and maroon as it retreated into the earth. I was exhausted from the weekend's races and travels. Sleep came expediently.

* * *

I arrived at Boone's local "weekend worlds" group ride at the renowned The Track Stand bike shop on a cool May morning. The Track Stand would have been well known, albeit just for its superb service and selection of bicycles, but the shop set itself apart from the pack with its second-floor café and coffee shop. Such a combination would be enough to attract most cyclists in the area, but many locals frequented the café for its quality eats and diverse imported beers.

Breathing the cold crisp air, I felt like the same person, but something was different. Friends, fellow racers, and even the local Fred riders seemed to greet me with an air of respect. People I didn't really know were coming up to me during the ride, congratulating me on my fourth place at collegiate nationals. I didn't know what changed; all that was different was a number, fourth, tenth, twenty-eighth: it was all the same to me. I wanted the top three.

Three hours into the ride came the famous Johnson River sprint. Hotly contested as "The Sprint," winning the race to the bridge was sometimes regarded in greater light to local riders than an actual race win, depending on the mix of riders. The lead-up to the sprint only had a small climb, half a mile; but coming only three miles from the sprint, it helped separate the pack and keep the sprint safe. This week's sprint featured its usual posse of local heroes, but included a number of professional riders in the area for the two National Racing Calendar criteriums next week.

* * *

Still on good form from nationals, I wanted to redeem my performance and pull off a good sprint. I always enjoyed the field sprints because of their chaotic nature and the need to process immeasurable conditions while finding the path of least resistance. I don't know why but I was always good at reading a sprint. I think it came from all the track racing I did growing up, but it's also an instinct. During the forty-five-mile-an-hour sprints, your brain processes so much information, but your mind can't react to all the information—that is left up to one's instinct. You can develop your instinct to a point, but you've either got it or you don't.

Passing over the top of the climb, the group split into a small field of twenty-some-odd riders. The pros quickly took to the forefront and led the charge for the line. Leading the split was the Alcatel team with four riders. I focused myself, turned off the reasoning part of my brain, tightened my grip on the handlebars, and let the instinct flow.

I started off toward the rear of the field but still within striking range of the front considering the more than two miles left to go. Out the corner of my eye, I saw it, a flash of a jersey, and I just jumped. Immediately I was on the express line, using a rider who thought he could out-power four professionals. As quickly as his burst of speed began, it was fading. I glanced to my left and nudged my way into line, seven back from the front.

Leaning slightly to the left, I took account of the situation. Seven riders from the front, a four-teammate train, everyone in front of me without a lead out, and it's one mile to go … crunch time! There was a slight right bend leading up the bridge, so I knew I wanted to take it to the inside, but I needed to establish myself early, force someone in front of me to try to take the lead, and not lose his draft, then pass him and hope to take the Alcatel rider at the line.

Half a mile to go, I punched it. My legs pressed on the pedals, the arms tightened, and I gritted my teeth in pain. Quickly my effort was matched and bettered by a rider in front of me; the bait was taken. I eased up and took the wheel. Alcatel's designated sprinter was now fully committed and started to pull away. With the Alcatel rider on my left and the other rider right in front of me, I was protected from the wind but also boxed in. Only three hundred meters left to go and I was in trouble, but then a bit of luck happened: The Alcatel rider kicked on the overdrive and opened a small gap on the left—it was my chance!

I jumped the gap, almost not wide enough for my 44-centimeter bars, and accelerated into his draft. One hundred meters to go and there were only two of us in the sprint; everyone was left behind. Fifty meters to go, I was pulling up beside him. At the finish I threw my bike. I lost.

I coasted on for about a minute, letting the group recollect. All I felt was the artery in my neck pounding away as I gasped to breathe. I started to fade to the back, getting some nice pats on the back for my daredevil bit of sprinting and giving the pro a run for his money. Everyone seemed slightly surprised. Everyone but me.

It was then I heard a voice say, "Good job, Mr. Bennet."

I looked to my right to see an older gentleman, aged, with tan but lightly blemished skin pulled taut over stringy muscles. His brown, slightly gray-streaked hair protruded out of an old-school hairnet helmet. His eyes gleamed with a sharpness of age but his smile was weightless as a teenager's. I recognized him; he was Jurgen Van Roy. I didn't know much about him other than seeing him around at some of the races and the fact he owned the bike shop from where the ride started.

"That was a spectacular sprint you just displayed; a little gutsy, but where would anyone get in this world without some guts?"

I stared at him for a second, opened my mouth, but nothing came out. Realizing quickly I hadn't said anything, I uttered, "Oh yeah, thanks … it was fun."

"Fun you say? Do you realize how close at the end you came to clipping another rider's wheel? You easily could have gone down."

"Really? Close? I saw the gap and took it; anyways, there was plenty of room. I punched it, but held off for a split second; most riders will just freak out over someone shooting a gap like that, so I knew chances were the rider next to me would brake, which he did, then I kicked it up into high gear. But even if he didn't back down I probably still had time to slow down."

"You realized all that during the sprint? You thought that through?"

"Nope, I just did what I knew to be the right way to go. I wouldn't call it thinking, just reaction … cause and effect."

"Well, that is interesting. Andy, do you have any racing plans for the summer?"

"No, not really."

"Well, would you like to come by the shop on tomorrow at 6 p.m.? I run a small amateur squad outta the shop; your collegiate coach Tony is the director and he has recommended we pick you up for the summer. We hit up most of the larger races on the East Coast, pick up the entry fee, all hotel, and all the gas; you are responsible for food. So you interested?"

"Oh yeah, I'm really interested! That would be perfect 'cause I didn't know what I was going to do this summer. Thought about just hanging around here and doing some local racing, but this sounds like a much better plan."

"Okay, we'll see you tomorrow."

We finished our conversation just as the pack rolled into the shop's parking lot. I said goodbye to Jurgen and rode off back to my apartment. I felt a nice feeling of satisfaction knowing what I would do for the coming months; beyond that I felt unsure, but my doubt was covered by the excitement of a summer of nothing but travel and racing.

* * *

Cruising over to The Track Stand, I was worried, excited, and anxious. Dismounting my city cruiser, I was greeted by Jurgen at the door of the shop.

"How do ya do, Andy?"

"Just fine, a bit sore from the week's riding but excited to hear about the summer racing plans."

Jurgen went on to list the guys racing for the summer. I knew all the guys on the team; they were the local hammerheads, guys who could light it up when they needed to but just weren't professionals due to various reasons.

Track Stand Racing, the team's official name, was lead by Dave Smith, a hard man if you ever met one. In his early forties, he spent more of his younger years on a bike than I have years. Short, dusty brown, military-cut hair neatly slicked forward and his slim build give him a natural appeal as a leader. Matching his appearance, his demeanor was professionalism personified. He and Jurgen became friends during his racing times here in the U.S. and the one season he spent abroad racing in Europe. He has long since hung up his carrier as a full-time cyclist and manages Jurgen's shop along with his duties in helping to run the team.

The rest of the team included Tim Langly, Brian Forbes, and Mark Winters. Tim was the eternal amateur: approaching his mid-thirties he had never ridden for a professional team, but has been a Category One rider for as long as most anyone can remember. He spends his year working odd jobs during the winter and races all summer long, living off of his cut of the race winnings.

Brian works as a professional tile layer, skilled at what he does and good at his work; but in his early twenties he picked up cycling after a running injury and advanced quickly to become one of the best riders in the area. Now at twenty-eight, he's at a critical point where he needs to decide what direction he wants to take his cycling: recreational or professional.

Lastly there was Mark, whom I knew from my college team and was a good friend. He is finishing his third year at Appalachian State University for Architecture and has taken off the summer from school to race with the team.

Jurgen motioned to me.

"Let's go inside and wait for the rest of the guys to show up. Cyclists never seem to make it anywhere on time."

Sure enough, the meeting started fifteen past the hour. After asking who would like some coffee, Jurgen began to address the group while pouring our coffee.

"Everyone, thanks for coming. I don't want to take up too much of your time, so we will try to keep this brief. This summer I will have Track Stand Racing represented by everyone here. I wanted to pool the talent of this area and give some of those pro teams a run for their money, kinda like Mr. Bennet did yesterday."

Suddenly realizing what was said, I thought about the need to react, but Dave continued where Jurgen left off.

"I'm sure Andy will have no problem holding his own, just as the rest of you should have little problem. If we didn't think you could handle this, we wouldn't have brought you here."

Jurgen continued without a pause.

"That's right. I want everyone here to be able to experience what it is like to travel and race with professionalism. This is why I have secured us sponsorship for the summer, team vehicles, and brought on Tony to be the team director. Along with Tony, Dave here will be your point man when it comes to team issues. He has invaluable experience and knowledge when it comes to racing. Learn from him. He can teach you more this summer than you have ever learned in all the years leading up to now." Jurgen motioned to Tony. "I don't really have much to add; just that I would like for everyone here to take their game up another level. We have the resources for success, so let's not waste them."

It was pretty much left at that. Jurgen distributed papers with our race schedule and the places we would be racing.

Riding home, I pondered what would come from the summer, and my mind drifted into contemplation as it often does while on the bike. I let an insidious grin broaden across my face as I thought of the possibilities that lay before me. I was starting something great yet obscure.

* * *

"Tim! Let's get to the front. Andy, follow us now!"

Most who would hear such force in a voice would think it crude, but from Dave it was done with an air of style that brought subtle softness, and those to whom it was directed were unconsciously subservient. It was a good thing we were on his side too; the timing couldn't have been any better. Just as we made our way to the front of the field, the pace quickened and pain increased.

Just over seventy minutes into the Claredon Cup Criterium, a small, two-man break had a thirty-second lead. Containing an Alcatel and a Xerox rider, this left out the other two of the big four quartet, Merrill Lynch and Nissan/Bianchi. For any break to succeed, at least three of the four were needed, and right now the Merrill Lynch and Nissan/Bianchi boys were at the front, charging hard. As the pace quickened, the peloton began to string out over the short one-kilometer course. I was glad for Dave's advice because right now I was on the tail end of the "safe-zone" of the field. Everyone to the rear of me was doomed to the eternal yo-yo effect, wherein the speeds going into a corner slowed down to a pitiful twenty mph then accelerated to the upper thirties to play catch up for the speed previously lost. Right now I was saving incomputable amounts of energy over the riders behind me, and I was grateful because it was killing me just to stay toward the front.

"Five laps to go, riders. Five laps to go," bellowed the announcer over the speakers. Looking up the road, I could just see the two breakaway riders in the corner, less than ten seconds up the road. They were doomed by the increasing speed and were going to be swallowed up in the next two laps.

I looked around to assess the situation, mark the well-known sprinters and their locations, who has teammates near, and watch for a pattern to the seemingly spasmodic flow of the race. The course was a difficult one because the last turn was dangerous with a slightly off-camber corner to the left just two hundred meters before the finish line. Having gone through at least fifty times so far in the race, I noticed a nice line to the inside, but there was a problem. To hit the line right, you needed to take a far outside line to cut the corner, and this left you open on your inside left. If someone was to cut on your inside, you had the choice of crashing or going wide, and possibly crashing on the off-camber corner. Unconscious thinking told me the risk was worth the benefit; the decision was made.

Three to go and the field was just coming together, but not for long. The promoter had gone out and challenged the crowd to raise a bounty for the "gambler's prize": the first rider to cross the line with one lap to go. At last note the prime was a tad over four hundred dollars, and going under the motivation of "no cash, no food," I had my sights set on winning the prize.

Going into a left corner with two and a half laps to go I noticed a rider on my left forcing his way through the field. It was one of the Merrill Lynch riders, Bobby Thompson, who was a well-known track rider from Australia. I obliged to his not-so-subtle, forceful requests to get through the field, not out of fear, but to let him take charge of the attack. There was no way I was going to drive it solo all the way, but if I could get towed to the line I would have a chance. Sure enough he bolted up the left side before the final corner, and with another rider in tow I was able to jump on for third spot.

Driving the pace all the way for the next lap, Bobby kept the pace high. He was well known for his final burst of speed, and I knew I needed to take the lead before the final corner. This was going to call for some uncommon and slightly insane tactics on my part. The lead-up to the finish had three turns, one ninety degrees right-hand, and then two consecutive ninety-degree left-hand corners. Going into the right-hand bend, I was still in third, but with some substantial force against the pedals I accelerated around the second rider on his left and took the inside corner from him.

In cycling, going into any cornering situation, no matter the size of the riders involved, the rider with his handlebars in front of the other rider has control of the rider behind him. The problem arises when two riders go into a corner side by side and fight for control of the line. Those are the times when crashes happen.

I dove into the corner and wanted to carry my speed and catch Bobby by surprise so he wouldn't have time to react, and by taking the shorter line to the inside I started to overtake him. Before he realized what had happened, I was in control and leading through the corner, forcing him to take the outside line and to slow down. Hands down he was a better sprinter, but my expectation was that he wouldn't carry as much speed as I was and I could grit it out to the line.

Pushing with everything I had in my body, I held nothing back. Peripheral vision became a blur and instinct took over. Tensioned arms pulled the handlebars as my legs pounded out all their strength through the cranks. As I saw the line approaching, I threw my bike to ensure the victory as the final-lap bell rang loudly.

Crossing the line, I noticed Bobby next to me on my right. I couldn't tell who had won; I wasn't looking for him, as I was lost in the pain of lactic acid euphoria. That was it for me. I let the rest of the race fly past me as the big-four quartet and others battled it out for the win. I cruised the last lap pondering what my next meal would be: Ramen noodles or a nice quarter cut of steak?

Rolling over to the team van, I saw Tony by the side of the road and slowed down to talk to him. He seemed pleasantly pleased with my performance, even a bit more hyper than normal. It was then I felt a hand grip the back of my neck.

Just as I swung my head to see who it was I heard the thick Aussie accent, "Crikey mate, that was some of the most stupid insane shite I have ever seen pulled by a rider this year. You sure got some bollocks on ya, mate. Don't know whether I should praise you or just deck you right here for pulling that one on me, but anyways, you pulled if off quite well, mate. Goodonya!"

I stood there, my mouth gaping open, with wide, puzzled eyes. Before I could utter a word he started to roll off. Tony, just as flabbergasted as I, said only, "Well, I guess that means you got the sprint. Dave pulled off a nice result too; fifth with Tim in tow for ninth. So we made bit of cash for the day. I have to say this was our best result so far."

I followed Tony over to the van, and the team gathered for a small debriefing of the race. It was our shortest speech of the season from Dave, as we didn't have any need to analyze a laundry list of mistakes, but the short and sweet praise for a day's job well done. I felt it then, the feeling of success. It started in the miniscule fibers of hairs of my neck and spread across my entire body. I was tired, but I didn't feel that way. I felt like I could take on the world.

* * *

Back at the hotel I stepped out of the shower to hear a knock-knock on the door, and I yelled at Mark to get the door. In walked Tony.

"Boys, we got a little treat tonight. I ran into the Xerox team in the lobby and we are going to join them for dinner down the road at a little Italian bistro. It's a treat, on Jurgen. I talked to him on the phone and he said it was time you guys had a nice meal, especially after such a beautiful performance. Be ready at seven thirty sharp in the lobby; casual dress with team polos will work just fine."

Jurgen was right; we had been running on empty the last couple of weeks. The first couple of races of the season were utterly uneventful. Dave pulled off the expected upper-echelon placing of a seasoned rider, but the rest of us all floundered as pack filler. Today's result was a breakthrough ride for both Tim and me. I was relieved to finally have something to tell the 'rents other than, "I'm fine, racing is fun, it was really hard." I could now show some monetary gain for the pain.

Down in the hotel lobby we all gathered and greeted the other riders as Dave introduced everyone to each other. Dave was the best bridge to the pro peloton one could ask for; his clout and respect earned over the years of racing gave weight to our team that no results could achieve. I was familiar with almost every one of the Xerox riders in attendance that night. In fact, there were a few of them who had been in the sport so long that they adorned the walls of my bedroom when I was growing up. I was a bit starry-eyed but just happy to see myself among people as passionate as I was about cycling.

The walk down to the bistro was short, and while walking I noticed Frank Williams come into stride beside me.

He leaned over and said, "Hey, didn't you win the gambler's prize today?"

"Um, yeah ... that was me."

"That was a gutsy and aggressive move."

"Thanks!"

"I'm Frank Williams."

"I know that ... everyone here knows that. I'm Andy Bennet."

"Oh sorry, some people just look so different in regular clothes that you can't sometimes tell. It's good to meet you, Andy."

Everyone knew Frank Williams; he was one of those guys who was on my wall growing up. His top credit was winning the USPRO championships six years ago in a wonderful solo victory in Philadelphia. I watched that race from the sidelines and it was something else. Frank is still one of the top-placed riders in the U.S.

The conversation with Frank flowed all the way to the bistro, and before I knew it, we had dessert in front of us, empty bottles of wine in front of the coaches and staff, and conversations emanating everywhere. The conversation with Frank migrated through various areas of interest until we ended up on the subject of why.

Frank, with overemphasis by the use of talking hands, asked, "So Andy, why do you do it? Why do you ride your bike?" I looked at him dead in the eyes and said nothing.

"What? No reason? There is always a reason to everything. Sometimes we see the reasons, but don't say anything. Other times we don't know they are there, but feel them. The other times the reason lurks in the consciousness of the mind but is hidden by misperception, people, and ideas. So don't worry if you don't know why."

I didn't understand him, so I replied back with a question. "Well, why do you ride a bike?"

Frank stared directly at me, tilted his head back slightly, and raised an eyebrow while exposing a few teeth.

"I ride because I love the pain."

Perplexed I muttered, "Pain? What do you mean, pain?"

"Just what I said: I enjoy pain."

"And how did you figure this out?"

"It was seven years ago, during Paris-Roubaix, section fourteen of the race's cobbles. I was riding in the lead group when I had a front flat and crashed. When I righted, a Mavic neutral support mechanic put a new wheel on my bike, and the feeling of intense pain throbbed in my hand. I started to chase and the pain began to grow. It was then I said, "Fuck it!" and put my head down and let the pain escape me. I started to feed off of it; the more it hurt the harder my legs went. I thought for a moment my legs had reached their limits, but I dug deeper. Not only did I make it back on, I was able to still place in the top ten. After the race the team doctor came over to examine my hand. Turns out I had broken two fingers and some other smaller bones. I realized then why I ride a bike: no normal person would do this sport."

My jaw felt too heavy to pull up the exposed gap between my lips. Awestruck understated the way his words affected me.

All I could utter was, "Pain?"

"Children from a young age are taught that pain is a bad thing. You hit your hand, it hurts, so don't hit it again. But cycling is all about pain; you can't win a race without the burn, the piercing feeling of lactic acid invading your muscles. Cycling is all about teaching your body to deal with pain, then accept pain, and finally to think of pain as good."

"So you learned all this from Paris-Roubaix?"

"Paris-Roubaix isn't a race for even two percent of the professional peloton; it's a different breed from them all. What I realized was a focal point of my time in Europe."

"So Europe taught you who you were on a bike?"

A heaving of air erupted from his chest as he let out a large and long chuckle. An astute feature of serenity spanned his face as he said, "I learned a lot of things in Europe. … Why I ride a bike was just one of them."

I stared at him and he smiled, "Andy, this was a good conversation tonight. I look forward to seeing you around at the races this season." Frank turned to answer a question from a teammate.

I started to play with my chocolate cake in front of me with my fork and stared at the table. The way he described his reasoning made sense in my head. The sadistic nature of the reasoning aside, it was the closest assertion to the rationale behind my obsession with cycling. I didn't know what it was, but I could feel something being awoken from the reality of the words.

* * *

Track Stand Racing arrived at the Fitchburg Stage Race, a small three-day event in Fitchburg, Massachusetts, with high hopes. The first two days went well for the team, but no one found himself in the overall standings. Tony started into one of his pre-race rants that started off even-tempered then snowballed faster and faster as his natural excitement pushed the words closer and closer together.

"Guys, we have had some real breakthrough rides in the past month; we are approaching the end of July, and the respect we earned is starting to fade away. You may look at the last two days as a failure, but let's take the problem and use it to our advantage. Since no one here is within striking distance of the overall victory we will go after the stage win. Follow those first breaks, kill those legs of yours, there is nothing left to save for today. Watch and listen, stay to the front. Every other guy in the peloton who isn't in the top ten is in our position and has the same idea, so play your cards at the right moment."

I hated to agree with Tony's statements; the truth hurt sometimes, but you just had to deal with it and move on. I missed the taste of success, as did everyone around me. We wanted more, and this was a great chance. The day's race was eighty miles and we were enough in number that if we didn't do something, we shouldn't even be called cyclists.

Starting the race, I saw Frank Williams as he greeted me during the neutral roll out. He was wearing the leader's jersey after dominating the first day's road race and keeping all attempts at the throne at bay during the criterium the second day.

"Hey, Andy, you ready for a bit of fun?"

"Don't you mean some pain?"

"Like I said, a bit of fun!"

I grinned at him, nodded, and then started to weave my way further up the field. In another minute the neutral roll out was over and the lead car waved the green starter's flag.

The attacks came immediately and everyone was there to cover them. Brian Forbes was the first to make a breakaway attempt stick. He rolled away like a locomotive and never looked back. He could power away like no one I ever knew, but just had one really good pace: super fast. He was not the smartest rider, and his strength came from pushing the pace others couldn't hold. The field pursued him in angst for a good thirty minutes before he was reeled back to the peloton. As fast as it happened he tried again, but Dave let out a quick yell, "Brian, not again; give it a bit of a rest, hide, then make another go of it all." Brian slowed down and faded into the peloton.

It was go time. I was on full alert and I had backup from Dave, just in front of me, and Mark, who was on my right about two riders over. Dave yelled back to me, "Andy, get ready to counter."

I nodded, not wanting to break my rhythm in breathing, then looked over my right to Mark. I made eye contact and he immediately knew the score. Unspoken communication was the advantage of getting to consistently race and travel with a team. We all began to know each other's thoughts like an old married couple. I started to nudge my way to the front as Mark did the same.

Dave took account of our positions and started to attack, bringing a couple of riders with him. Mark and I latched onto the single-file train that formed as racers struggled to gain any draft advantage to alleviate the increasing drag. Dave did a spectacular job forcing riders into hurt, and as soon as he pulled off from his pull only two other riders were willing to fork over their energy in earnest to try to break the chain that protruded from the front of the peloton. Once their efforts were over, it was time. I started the counter.

The roads were undulating, the surface pristinely smooth asphalt, the leaves were luscious with the greens of summer, but I couldn't have told you any of those details at that moment. All I remember from the moments when I push the pace is a blurred peripheral vision and a focal point of a road passing beneath rotating wheels as sweat rolls down my face and the swelling sensation of pain. It's been described as tunnel vision, but it's not quite that, as the peripheral world is still known, just not consciously. I return to a state of consciousness as soon as the pressure on the pedals is lessened; in all, less than a minute has passed, but I couldn't tell.

Mark pulled up as I faded back. "Damn—Andy!" was all he could utter between deep heaving breaths. I was surprised when after only seven guys there was no one. I glanced back to see the peloton strewn across the road, indifferent to chase the motley group of riders in front of them. I sprinted into last place and set into my rhythm as I lowered my heart rate from the previous effort.

Breakaways were tricky and this was no different. There we were, eight guys, all of us with one thing on our mind: the win. At first the pace started to fluctuate radically and I was put into a spot of bother.

I couldn't stand it any longer and finally barked out at the riders, "Damn it, guys! Who's here to win and who's here to fail? Keep it steady! I like the odds of eight guys instead of 125! Keep it steady!"

I came across a bit tyrannical, but it did the job needed and the group started into a cohesive rhythm through the course. I was putting in some hard pulls at the front of the break, as I didn't want this to fail. Mark made some comment on saving energy, but I didn't listen. I was keen on driving this to the end.

After about thirty minutes of the breakaway I heard a beep-beep at the rear. It was Tony in the team car, head protruding from the window, yelling up at the break, "You're up two minutes on the field, and they're just keeping tempo. Keep up the pace and the break will be able to last to the end!"

Two minutes wasn't enough for me. I continued with my pace making at the front.

The steady rhythm of the break allowed me to relax, let my mind drift as I followed the wheel in front of me and the miles rolled on by without much comprehension of the time. I didn't notice the bulk of the breakaway attempt while my mind was occupied by the monotonous consistency and my compulsive desire to have it succeed.

I didn't realize how far we were into the race until the break hit a short climb and an unknown rider decided it was time to go solo. My mind lapsed out of its lull and expediently followed the countermoves of the attack. From this point it was on like Donkey Kong, and I looked around for Mark. I knew we were in our final lap, but I wasn't sure how far from the finish we were and asked, "Mark, what's left in the race?"

"About ten miles, the attacks are going to start coming every which way; we need to look out!"

By this point in the season, both Mark and I knew this and it should have gone without saying, but I just nodded my head and looked around to gauge the situation, which was not too bad.

We had two out of the eight, and there were at least three other guys who were as tired as I was, so I liked the odds. I looked over at Mark, gave him a small nod, and he knew I was ready. I watched as Mark launched a mother of an attack across the road on the left-hand side, his bike swaying side to side as his arms guided the handlebars to control the fury of the two piston legs pressing the pedals. Quickly Mark established a gap and had two other riders hanging on to the back of his wheel. I looked around at blithe faces staring back at me. No one wanted to commit his energy to the chase.

This is the hardest part of a race for most people: the determining of where to use what precious energy they have left in the most effective manner. I was in a good situation, along with another rider, as we had teammates up the road, thereby negating our obligation to pursue. I watched the other three riders and waited. Like clockwork one of the rider's anticipation took hold. He couldn't let any more distance be gained and started an attack. I jumped on to chase, third in line, and held on as they went after the lead break.

As the rotation of the riders started, I skipped out on my pulls at the front, much to the dismay of my associates in the break. Lots of not-so-nice things were being said about me being a slacker, someone who doesn't want to win, but I didn't care. It was all a stupid tactic for people too stupid to know it was a stupid tactic. Yelling would not win a race unless your mouth spontaneously started to power your quads.

After a solid five minutes of chasing, the two lead groups were less than fifty meters apart and within three miles of the finish. I knew I was feeling good, and there was no sign of the field behind us. The time was fast approaching to play my cards and I was ready to lay the smacketh down!

The last three miles were a bit hilly, the perfect place to accelerate around a corner or up a slight rise, put some extra lactic acid in the legs of everyone, and see who can take the pain. Just as the five of us caught the lead group of three, I wasted no time in going on the offensive. Utilizing a short, sharp rise, I let the throttle on the legs open to full, put down the head, gritted the teeth, and went into the zone. Pain began to come in waves across my legs as they tried and tried to constrict to stop the pain, but I wouldn't let them. I just told them to shut up and kept going.

I pulled off to the side to see who endured, and was disappointed to find three other riders on my wheel, but no Mark. I didn't like how much effort was put into the attack only to lose four riders, including a teammate. It was too late to worry about that now; time to make do with what I had. I accelerated onto the back of the break and started to plan.

I glanced back after the next pull and the riders behind were disorganized; not too much chance of them chasing back. I looked at the guys around me: one professional and two amateurs, and not one I recognized, so I didn't know what I was up against. The pro rider with the Merrill Lynch team looked to be fresh and wasn't a small guy, so I had to guess he was the guy to beat. Just as I came to the back of the group I saw the one-mile-to-go banner, and the spectators were filling the roadside with cheers. The time was at hand.

I muscled my way in behind the Merrill Lynch rider and prepared for the sprint. It was then I felt it, a little bobble of the rear wheel. I didn't think much until the next corner came and it felt like I was riding on a Slip-N-Slide. I looked down at my rear wheel; it was going flat! Shit, shit, shit was all I could think. Of all the times and all the places, why now!

Right then one of the amateur riders attacked when he noticed me bouncing my rear wheel. Quickly all three riders were gone, and I sprinted after them in vain. I could see the finish line, the riders were mere meters in front of me, but I couldn't catch them. All I could do was just ride out the flat, hope the tire didn't roll off, and get to the finish line before the rest of the break caught me.

I came across the line while the announcer made some stupid comment about how much of a crapshoot a bike race can be. I headed straight to the team van. Fourth place again. I felt like I was Ullrich at the Tour, condemned to always be one place from that which I desired.

Tony arrived quickly, looked at me, looked at the bike thrown to the side of the road, and just shrugged. I just sat there on the curb, water bottle in hand, with no expression on my face. Internally I was pissed off beyond belief, but I didn't want anyone else to know. All I was going to hear for the next hour was the banter of people with the great "aww, you coulda" talk that always accompanies such bad luck.

Tony picked up on my mood and let me be. I saw Mark roll up and asked how he did. Turned out he picked up fifth place in the race. The results looked good on paper, but they should have been better. The field rolled in a few minutes after the first rider and the rest of the team showed up soon enough. I spent the next half hour re-explaining the same damn thing over and over to everyone. I was actually not too annoyed until Dave came up and said, "Hey, man, cheer up; later tonight we will be at your parents' house and you can visit with them."

I had almost forgotten about the visit to my parents. The team's budget was at Ramen noodle levels at this point in the season, so we were going to stop at my parents' house for the day on our way back to North Carolina. I've always had a great relationship with my parents and love them to death. There was just one problem: the consistent bombardment of questions and pressure to do something with my life and pick a major in school. They knew I raced a bike, but really didn't know much about bike racing. To them, it was just a hobby I did, something like little league baseball to be outgrown for more adult hobbies like working a nine-to-five job. I regretted each call home for the simple fact I was talking to people who were supposed to know me best yet knew me very little.

I changed clothes, washed up, and packed my stuff up with the rest of the team. Lethargically, I crawled into the team van and sat next to the window, pressed my head onto the window, and drifted away into internal reflection.

II—Vacuous Dreams

We arrived late in the night and my mother, Mary, was still up reading a book. I quickly introduced everyone on the team and then headed to my old bedroom. I lay there in my bed, eyes open, with questions running through my head. I tried to take my mind off all the "what if" questions of life by counting the number of little bumps on the textured ceiling. Eventually I drifted into sleep, but there wasn't much restful sleep that night. I guess my subconscious knew more than my mind was willing to admit.

The next morning I was awakened by the thumps of feet on the hardwood floors and the pungent aroma of strong coffee. I threw on a pair of pants and a T-shirt and rolled out of bed and down to the kitchen. I was starving from the day before because I was a bit too pissed off to eat all of my dinner. I came around the corner to find Dave and Tony sitting around the table with Simon, my father. I saw his mood; it was typical of his nature: straightforward, with the questions that mattered to him only, mostly money related. I walked over to the coffee pot and poured myself a cup while listening to the conversation.

My father rattled on, "Well, Dave, that sounds like one interesting summer; so how did you guys come out this summer?"

"As I was just saying, the team had some good results, including your son here."

Tipping his coffee cup in my direction as I started to sit down, he said, "He's a real animal in the peloton."

"Oh, I was talking about money; you guys make anything this summer doing those bicycle rides?"

I caught Tony and Dave's glances as I raised my coffee for my first, warm sip, precariously replying by raising my eyebrows amidst the cup's simmering steam.

Tony interjected, "Track Stand Racing came out okay; we made back most of what we put in this summer. For us it's not about the money; it's getting guys like your son to NRC races so they can see the upper level of racing in the Northeast."

My father looked at him for a second. "So you pretty much broke even. Guess that is okay."

I knew something like this was going to happen, but I wasn't expecting it at such an early hour, before I was able to function well enough to assist in moving the conversation along to another subject. My luck was with me this morning, much more than the previous day, as my mother entered the room and asked what everyone would like for breakfast. Dave quickly got up to help her prepare the breakfast despite her protests that she didn't need the help. I just relaxed and enjoyed my coffee while my father started talking to the other guys entering the kitchen, beckoned by the smell of bacon.

Shortly after our late breakfast, we all suited up for a little spin around my old stomping grounds. I took the team out and back on a short, forty-mile route I always enjoyed riding growing up. It included three hard hills, the last of which up Hager road was almost one mile long and a steep son of a gun. The ride went very well, and I surprised myself at how easily I made it over the Hager Road climb. It had been at least a year since I had done the climb, but I never expected to ascend the climb with such ease of effort.

Back at the house, I took a quick shower, went down to the living room, and started to visit with the parents. I asked how the neighbors were doing, old friends from school, and how my dad was doing at the bank. He was the manager of a small but successful bank in a small suburb of Allentown, hence his preoccupation with money and business. His world revolved around selling the business of money to people who had money from business. Soon enough a question came along and caught me off guard.

My dad asked, solemnly, with a directness of a supervisor leading an employee to make the more correct choice, "So what classes are you going to be taking this next semester? Registration is starting at most of the colleges around here and you don't want to get stuck in Basket Weaving 101 now."

I didn't know what to reply. I hadn't thought about school; it seemed as if it was a lifetime ago. The last two and a half months had come and gone faster than I ever thought. School was the furthest subject from my mind at this point, and I had no answer. I blurted out, "Guess I'll take a math class, one more science to finish up the core requirement, and then two others. I don't know. I haven't thought about school much this summer."

Simon replied, "Well, you need to start to think about your future. That teammate of yours, umm ... Mark, yeah. He will be an architect next year after he graduates. That is a good job; he will have a nice, secure future."

I hated the way my father made everything about money, success on his terms, and respectable occupations.

Ardently I said, "Well, some of us don't want school or money. Some of us want to be happy with our lives!"

The reaction couldn't be calculated by any measurement known to man. My father's brain sat there, churning my statement over and over in his head, coming up with an error message. In his world, without money there would never be happiness. My mother's book lowered to her lap as she stopped her half-reading, half-listening act and stared bewildered at me past her thin-framed reading glasses resting evenly on the end of her nose. I looked at each of them, back and forth, waiting for a reaction.

Finally, after a seemingly long amount of time, my father let out a sullen sentence: "What kind of future can you have in bicycles?"

I looked him straight in the eye, "I know what I want; I want to ride my bike."

"But what about a future? College will give you a future. I talked to Tony and Dave this morning; there isn't any money in cycling."

"There is money in Europe!"

"What now, are you moving to Europe?"

In my mind it just clicked. Europe, why not? Europe was a place spoken about reverently; the awe of words rolling from those who had been there and come back carried the allure of the world's greatest tale ever told. I didn't know a lick about Europe, but I knew I wanted to be there.

"I will go to Europe. Over there you can be a rider and a success."

My dad and mom just couldn't believe what they were hearing. My moving to Boone for school was a huge issue; now here I am, telling them I am going to Europe! I felt scared of what their reaction would be. Simon let out a large sigh that effortlessly rolled into a lecture on the repercussions of such an action.

"Andy William Bennet, there is no reason to go to Europe, no reason to continue to ride a bike. You need to finish up school and find a career. Playing around on your bike won't get you anywhere. But if you insist on continuing such nonsense, you will be on your own. You shouldn't expect any financial help from us. Try to see where your bicycle can take you then."

I looked at these people in front of me; they seemed not to be parents, but dictators. I let out a snide remark, "Shall I just turn off my brain and let you live my life? 'Cause you seem to know me better than I know myself."

With that, I just got up and left. I couldn't take it all. The assault on cycling as worthless was an assault upon me. They could never understand the symbiosis between a rider and a bike. I went upstairs and started to pack my bags for the trip back to Boone. Once that was done, I just walked to the back porch and sat on a lawn chair. I watched the crimson sun slowly sink into the silhouette of the horizon as I contemplated my life. The only other word spoken to my parents was "goodbye" when I left.

Back in Boone things were tense those first couple of days. I didn't get much sleep, but at least I got in some good riding. When the world seems too much to handle, I jump on my two-wheeled friend and let the problems fade away with the miles, and evaporate alongside the sweat exiting my pores. Some people go to confession; I leave my confessions to the open road: the world was my confessional.

As the miles rolled away, the idea of Europe become more and more appealing to me. I could think of almost every successful rider I knew and at least part of their past included Europe. I knew Dave Smith spent time there, and Frank Williams was a pro on a team over there and look at where he has gone. I remember watching tapes of the races in Europe, fans lining the road, standing all day just to get a glimpse of the riders. *La Grande Boucle*, the Tour de France, with roads lined for miles with crazed fans all over France. Those were the things of my dreams.

The end of the week came quickly. I had a message on e-mail from my dad, telling me I needed to register for college in the next week or my next month's rent wasn't going to be paid and there wouldn't be any grocery money in my bank account. I didn't want to deal with it all. The saving grace was a big barbeque that Jurgen was throwing at his house on Saturday. It was an end of the summer bash to celebrate the racing and finish off the summer racing the team had completed.

I arrived promptly at Jurgen's house at 5 p.m. but didn't find anyone from the team there. I went around back and greeted Jurgen, and he introduced me to his wife, Amy. I looked around and then said to Jurgen, "Where is everyone? I thought you said five."

"That I did. It's a little before five, but as I told you before, cyclists are always running fashionably late."

"Oh, well, is there anything I can help you guys with?"

"Not really. I think Amy might need a little help in the kitchen bringing out some of the food. Honey, you need any help?"

"Sure, I could use a little."

I followed Amy inside and helped to bring out the food. Soon enough everyone arrived and the party began.

After a feast of food, we all gathered on Jurgen's back porch around his fire pit. The summer sun was setting softly against the undulating silhouette of earth behind us as a cool breeze kept the summer heat at bay. It was a great relief to be around everyone without the pressures of racing. We just sat around, regaling exaggerated tales of the summers racing, antics pulled while off the bike, and all the good times. I just sat around, watching everyone's faces and their expressions. I couldn't believe all that we packed into one small summer as I experienced more this summer than I did in all the last year.

After laughing all night so hard that I swore my cheeks were going to be stuck in the grin position, the party started to die down. Slowly people started to leave, while Jurgen and I started a conversation. He was asking about the summer, how I liked the travel, and my thoughts on racing at a higher level. I could see it in Jurgen: He knew about my argument with my parents. Soon enough he let it out.

"So what is this I hear about you and your parents? Had a little disagreement, did you?"

I looked at him and slouched a little more in my chair. "Oh … that. It's nothing. They just want me to live a life I can't."

Jurgen sat up a little straighter, drank another swig of beer from a glass in his left hand. He exhaled a light breath and asked, "So what life do you want, Andy?"

"To be honest, I want to be a cyclist. I know it's not a practical thing to be; my dad is right about that, but I don't care about practicalities. I care about doing something I love, and I love riding my bike. This summer was the best thing I ever did in my entire life. If I could do this forever I would, but I will settle for as long as my body will allow me to. My father makes it all about money. I just want to have food to eat, a place to sleep, and as long as I am doing what I love I will be happy. Does anyone really need any more in life than that?"

Jurgen looked surprised, but not shocked like I suspected. "Well, cycling can be practical; there are many people out there, including myself, who made a decent living riding a bike, but you have to love it to make it work."

I looked at him very puzzled. "You raced a bike and made money?"

He let a little chuckle out, "Yes, I did. For eleven years I raced professionally in Europe. It wasn't the easiest way to make a living, but I wouldn't have done it any other way."

"Why hasn't anyone ever mentioned this to me?"

"I don't make it known; that and no one ever really asks. They just assume I have always been in cycling because of my shop. Anyways, people tend to treat you differently after they find out information like that; it's stupid because nothing really changes."

"It's funny you mentioned Europe. I told my parents I was going to go there. I said it mostly outta anger, to piss them off, but after I came back here it made more and more sense to me. I remembered talking to Frank Williams. You know him, the Xerox rider. He told me about his time there and it just stuck in the back of my head. I did a lot of thinking this week. I want to go there. I want to prove myself as a cyclist. I want to become a professional!"

Jurgen looked at me and pulled back his cheeks in a sly grin as his head nodded slowly. "Andy, there it is: the fire in you! I knew you had it in you; that is why I asked you to join the team for the summer. I saw that something, an untouchable, intangible, immeasurable quality in your spirit. You have it in you; you don't know it, but you have it. I can tell you now, you will hear these words and still not know it, but you will know it later."

He paused, smiling at the bewilderment in my eyes. "Europe, eh?"

"Yes, but … umm … I can't really go, I don't have the money. Plus I don't know thing one about getting there."

"Andy, tell you what. It's getting late and there's been enough talk this evening. How about you come by tomorrow at ten a.m.; we'll go for a ride and talk about this Europe thing you want to do. Okay?"

"Okay, ten a.m.?"

"Yes."

* * *

The sun was full past the mountains casting crisp shadows about the green foliage. I arrived at Jurgen's to find him outside waiting for me. He was on an old bike, probably from the eighties, but still in pristine shape with shiny chrome lugs. It was old-school and a testament to the personality of Jurgen. He was decked out in the Track Stand Racing kit, but had on a hair net.

I rolled up to him and asked, "So what's up with the hairnet? Not the safest helmet around?"

"True, but I don't plan on crashing today, do you?"

I laughed, "No … So where we heading to?"

"Well, I think it would be good to get in about three hours. As far as where, we will let the inner caprice dictate the path we take—no real plan today."

I nodded and then looked around. "So which way?"

"Choose one; they are all on roads, and some that I would be hard-pressed to call roads."

I thought for a second and decided to start toward hills. I felt like some hard riding today.

I didn't know what to expect. Jurgen just kept to himself for the first half hour, then once we started up the base of a light rise he asked, "Where would you like to go in Europe? There are many great places to choose from."

"I … I don't know, anywhere. I just want to race my bike."

"Well then, what about Belgium?"

"Belgium? Where Eddy Merckx is from?"

"Yes, Eddy and myself. I grew up there, raced most of my professional life in Belgium, and still have many friends over there. If I made the call, you would be in, which is one of the hardest hurdles: having an in. From there it will be up to you. I can bring you there; it's up to you to make it all work."

"You would do that for me. Why?"

"Like I said last night, the fire I see in you. Right now it is a small flame, confined by your doubt, but Europe has a way of fueling that type of flame and making it burn bright. Then again, Europe is a harsh world when it comes to racing, and all that it gives it can take. There has been many a rider who left Europe with a lifelong disdain for the bike, never to touch or ride it again. Are you prepared to venture into something that can break the very core of who you are?"

What was I to say? I didn't expect the talk to be this serious, this morbid, but it was. Audaciously I replied, "I know what I want. I want to ride my bike. I want to prove not to others, but to myself that I am good enough."

"Well then, I will do my part. I will help you, but it's your life; make what you will of it. You should really think about delaying your school for the moment if you are going to do this. School is important, but if you are going to do something this important you will need to follow it completely. You will need to show up in Europe ready to rip legs off."

"Jurgen, I thank you and all, but there is a problem in stopping school. I really can't afford to go to Europe. The reality of it all is I can't make it work, dollar-wise. My father is going to cut me off from all help if I stop school, and I don't have but maybe two hundred dollars to my name."

"Andy, I'll tell you this now and only once. In life, no matter the reason, don't let money get in the way of something you love. It's stupid. Money is important, but it isn't life. I have seen one too many people spend their lives in the pursuit of money only to have money in the end and have never lived. All they did was die monetarily wealthy, but far from rich where it counts."

"I know, I hate how my father holds money over me as leverage, but he knows how much it affects life and he will use it to get his way."

"All is not lost, Andy. Like I said, I will get you there. I tell you what; you will come live with me and work at the bike shop. That will actually be best. I can really watch over you this winter, help to groom your habits, and ensure you are on the right path … Yes, that is a brilliant idea. So what do you say?"

I couldn't believe this. I knew Jurgen, but I didn't know him and here he was bringing me into his home. "Umm … OKAY … I can't thank you enough. This is really a dream come true."

"Don't start practicing your victory salutes just yet; the dream hasn't even begun. First I want you to do something for me. I want you to call your parents. Calmly explain to them this plan, what you will be doing, and your reasons. They are still your parents and you will want them to understand you. They only do the whole money thing because they think school is best for you and they want the best for their boy. Okay?"

"I'll call when I get back."

"Okay then, let's enjoy the rest of the ride. Tell me some more about this summer. How did you like the racing?"

Jurgen and I conversed for another two hours about the summer's racing. We had only met a couple of times previously but he felt like a friend I had known for years. He was just one of those people you meet who you knew at hello. I arrived at home, put my bike against the wall of my apartment, and had never felt so alive in all my life as that one moment. All I could think was, "I can become a pro, a European pro." I think I fell asleep with a smile glued to my face.

* * *

The monotony of training is sometimes almost too much, but then again, consistency is the key to success, as Jurgen has been telling me. Each day for the last three months has almost been an exact repeat of the previous. The schedule is invariable, with the exception of the weekends, where my time on the bike was more and I was able to get in extra rest.

I was afforded a nice three-week break from the season after finishing up the racing year in late September. Jurgen wanted me to be able to get an early start on the year's training to give me more time to develop and not have to rush things. I had a vague idea of what I was going to be doing, but it wasn't anything like I had ever imagined.

The beginning of living with Jurgen was quite difficult. He would come knocking on the door of the guest room, my temporary abode at the moment, promptly at 6:30 a.m., and would drag me out of bed for some light stretching before breakfast. I have never been a morning person, but after some coercing with the promise of coffee, I found myself getting up without the aid of an alarm clock every day. Eventually, the light stretching turned into almost full yoga sessions three times a week. The other days would be filled with roller rides before breakfast to help cut down the winter fat.

Jurgen had some pretty drastic ideas about weight. There was one day I asked him if I should go to Tony at the university and get a body-fat test. He looked at me, laughed, and then just said, "Andy, you want the world's best body-fat test? Here ya go; take your fingers, pinch the back of your hand. Now, when you can do that on the rest of your body, you are at the right body fat!"

It was dramatic, but he was right. I did need to shed a few of those pounds of baby fat left over from my teens, but I was told not to worry.

With a sheepish grin, Jurgen explained, "This winter you will need some of that fat, but it will go away. You will ride so much that all you will want to do is sleep. All those miles will chisel you into a lean, mean cyclist, so weight will come off."

He was right: the weight was coming off and I was always tired. I never knew the body could feel the fatigue I was experiencing in my legs. I would come home from five hours in the cold, eat a bit of lunch, shower, take a quick nap for an hour, and then go over the shop to work till close. The first day I had a long ride, I showed up at the shop and was walking around the back, looking for something to do when Jurgen came in. He looked at me and started to shake his head.

"Andy, this piece of advice will help you survive this winter. You will be so tired in a few weeks and standing on your feet will do you worlds of harm. I want you to stay back here. Don't work the sales floor; just build bikes, true wheels and such from here."

Jurgen, pointing to a stool, continued. "Keep off your feet as much as possible. Let your legs rest. This is now your personal stool ... use it."

By this point in the training, I looked for that stool with the lust of a fourteen-year-old boy seeing a *Playboy* for the first time. The fatigue made me want to sleep all the time. When I was in school, my sleep patterns were all screwed up from cramming for tests then traveling on the weekends to races, and I had so much trouble trying to get to sleep because my body was put on such a sporadic schedule. Now when ten o'clock came I was in bed, asleep. No fuss, no muss. I slept well.

When I came home from the shop with Jurgen after closing, I would join him and Amy for dinner. She was such a wonderful cook, making the most delicious, healthy meals. She made sure I was eating right and would always put a little extra on my plate every time.

"Cyclists eat and eat, then eat some more, but you earned it and you need to replenish you glycogen for the next day's ride. Don't feel bad; us regular folk don't need so much to eat."

After pleasant conversation at dinner, I would watch a little TV while stretching, and wind down from the day, followed by a little massage to the legs to work out the sore spots, and I was off to bed.

Looking back, I was almost aghast at the changes I had made in my habits. Each and every change came with such gradual subtleness that I unconsciously assumed them. I thought of myself as an athlete before, but this was a level of commitment that left even me surprised. Despite all the monotony and consistency, each day was so much fun. Riding my bike gave me time to think, contemplate ideas and thoughts, and be by myself for a while. Working at the bike shop was also great. There were so many funny co-workers, and the barrage of stupid questions from customers always left a quirky smile on my face. Then came the dinners with Jurgen and Amy. Those were special times because I got to talk to Jurgen and begin to understand him.

Jurgen was the most fascinating guy I had ever met, but no one seemed to really know him. He was so quiet and reserved that most people assumed he had no opinion, but he chose his words as carefully as he chose those to whom to speak them. Other than myself, the only other person I had heard him speak to as bluntly was Dave Smith. Jurgen grew up in Oudenaarde, a small town in the Flanders region of Belgium. Apparently cycling was part of his family, as his father was a professional cyclist way back in the day. I recall hearing stories of carrying tubular tires and a wrench to switch gears. His brother was also a professional cyclist as he was and still lives in Belgium.

I was curious how this former pro cyclist from Belgium ended up in Boone, North Carolina. Jurgen, with a beer in hand called Westmalle Trappist in a special glass bearing its name, began to regale me in what he called "the greatest love story in bike racing." I could see a special gleam in his eye, and he talked with an air of excitement I rarely heard in his voice.

"That, Andy, is a wonderful story."

Looking at Amy, he said, *"Oh Schatje … Can I tell it?"*

She smiled and rolled her eyes a bit. "Sure, dear, but don't go on all night."

"Well, the year was 1989 and I was riding for the Panasonic Team in the Tour de Trump. It was later called the Tour Dupont and then faded away a couple years later. Anyways ... I was having a particularly good year results-wise and was very excited to come to the States. It was going to be my first time here, so I didn't know what to expect. So then ... oh yeah ... the Tour de Trump. Well, I ended up placing third on the second stage from Charlottesville to Petersburg, and I ended up in medical control. It was there that I met Miss Amy Marie Parker, an assistant to the medical staff, conducting the doping testing. I knew I had found the most special girl in the world when I saw her, but to say the least, it was a bit awkward when you're there to pee in a little bottle. The next day I ended up winning the stage and receiving the leader's jersey. I saw her again, but didn't work up the nerve to talk to her. I lost the jersey the next day on a hilly stage. I never was a good climber, but I ended up being called up for the random drug test three more times. After the third time I knew it wasn't just coincidence, and the final day of the race I worked up the courage to ask her to dinner. It was so great, and we just fell hard for each other. I ended up staying an extra week in the U.S. with her, then returned back after the race season to see her. We were married three months later. So that is how I meet Amy. We moved back to the U.S. after I finished up my career and settled here in Boone. So that is how I came to the U.S."

Jurgen's career fascinated me. I learned about his years in Europe. The people he met, places he visited, and races he had done. One cold winter day we went out for a ride and I asked, "So what was your favorite race ever?"

Jurgen smiled gently, his cadence paused in tandem with his internal reflection.

"Ronde van Vlaanderen. No question."

"Ronde van Vlaanderen? The Tour of Flanders?"

"Yes, the one and only. It holds a special place in my heart, like it holds in every racer from Belgium. Winning the Tour of Flanders is the dream of every young cyclist in Belgium. For me, I never won the Tour of Flanders, but one year I did place third. It was a great moment for me, and the memory of that result still brings chills to my spine. I still think about that race, what I could have done to win, but I knew I raced to my limit, then beyond it. I went on that year to win eleven races, but none were as sweet as third in the RVV. The Tour of Flanders is *haute catègorie*, not only in race rank, but also in the hearts and minds of Belgians. Win the Tour of Flanders and you are a god."

I couldn't believe the veneration in his voice, the crystal-clear precision and ease with which the memories poured from his mouth. I found the allure of the *Ronde van Vlaanderen* inspiring and used it. There were mornings it was cold outside, I was tired, and my bed beckoned me to stay snuggled up in a warm down comforter just a little bit longer, but I would arise, think of all the races Jurgen recounted, and used them to lure me to my bike. I would ride all by myself, but I would be surrounded by fellow racers in my mind, forcing breakaway attempts and letting races unfold in my head while I rode though the cold and rain. It kept the mind off of the realization of exactly how miserable it was outside. I did this for the whole winter.

In February things began to work their course. I was motorpacing behind Jurgen twice a week on the Green Machine, a rusty, green Honda Passport moped. It was a loud and whiny beast due to an exhaust pipe in disrepair. Still, once you got past the fumes, it was perfect for the job at hand. It would give you just enough draft to rest, but enough resistance to make you work: just what I needed.

I showed up at The Track Stand after a little two-hour spin to warm up the legs and prepared for our next motorpacing session. I walked in and said hi to everyone. I found Jurgen around the back with a large smile on his face. I was curious and asked, "So what's up with the big smile, Jurgen?"

"Not too much, just a bit of good news. I heard back today from a friend of mine in Belgium, Peter Ververken. He runs the BASE-Duvel team in Gent. He has a place for you to stay with some other foreign riders. You are set with a place to stay."

I couldn't believe what I was hearing. I wanted to jump up and down and scream I was so happy, but that would have been a bit too embarrassing, so I just quipped, "Oh, cool, that takes care of that problem."

Jurgen rebutted, "Yes, it does, but it's still a long way to go, so let's get you back on the bike and behind the motor. No sense wastin' time."

That day's motorpacing session, I was on fire. I was pushing it even harder, and Jurgen had to throttle the Green Machine for all it was worth just to keep me on my toes. He yelled out over the insidious whine of the motor, "Thought that bit of information would light the fire; let's use it! We'll tag on an extra thirty minutes!"

I nodded my head to him and we continued with the pacing. I had a new reason again to work hard, a place on a team in Europe! The reality of it all was setting in and left me high on possibilities.

Jurgen had barely turned off the motor when I began to unclip my helmet and ramble on, "So what's this team like? Who are they? What's the house like? Who are my teammates?"

Jurgen put his hand on my back and walked me to a table. "Andy, give yourself a bit of a rest; you're riding on an endorphin high."

"Oh, okay—So what's it all about? I want to know."

"Well, the team is BASE-Duvel, sponsored by a mobile phone and a beer company. Most of the riders are Belgian, but they do allow a couple of foreign riders on the team each year. Those riders all live in a small apartment above a bar that sponsors the team. In Belgium it's not one of the bigger teams like the Division III teams sponsored by their Division I counterparts, but they get invited to a lot of big races, including a few Interclub races. The apartment isn't the Hilton, but it is nice, has a washer and dryer, and is furnished. I worked out a deal with Peter for two hundred euros a month. Now this a good deal, and with what you have saved this winter you should be set financially for the year. See, I told you life isn't about money; you just need to have a little faith that it will work out and make it happen."

"Jurgen, how can I ever thank you?"

"Easy, *Breng enkele bloemen naar huis.*"

"What?"

"It's Flemish for 'bring home some flowers.' See, the winner of every race gets flowers."

"Oh, okay … I'll make sure to get some! This is all so cool. When do I leave?"

"Peter would like you there in first week of March so you can get used to the weather and be ready in April. The weather won't be great, but not too different from what it is here."

"Cool, I will start to look for a ticket today! … Uh, Jurgen, when should I get the return date for?"

"Your choice, Andy; you can stay as long as you want."

"I will stay the full season, no matter what!"

I knew not what was going to happen, but I knew I was going to stay. If there is one thing I will always do, it is stick something out to the end and give it my full effort. I had no reason, want, or need to stay in North Carolina, much less the U.S. I had this little apartment in Gent, Belgium, beckoning me. I felt the verge of greatness within my hands' grasp, standing mere inches away, with only a small forward movement on my part needed to lay claim to a dream.

The week before my flight I had restless nights. I wasn't worried, but excited about the great unknown that lay before me over on the other side of the ocean. I had heard stories of Europe, but what did it feel like? I was also a little nervous about my fitness. I was in great shape and the lightest I had ever been, but I hadn't been able to really test my form. The only race-like intensity I had in my legs was the bi-weekly motorpacing I did with Jurgen. I always felt nervous about the first race of the year, but now I was going to have to start the racing season in another country with abounding unknowns.

Despite my inability to sleep, the last week went by quickly due to all the pre-trip preparations. I was so worried about leaving something behind or forgetting something, like my bike. Thankfully, Jurgen was there as a voice of reason.

"Don't stress so much; all you need is your bike, your cycling shoes, passport, racing license, and everything else can be bought."

"Oh, okay, you are right."

"Just pack like you did for the summer of racing, add a little extra and your passport, and you got it all."

He was right once again. I knew what to do; I just needed to do it. I let the excitement of it all take over me. On the eve of my departure, I went out to eat with Jurgen and Amy at a local Chinese restaurant they both enjoyed. It was their treat to me before I left for my journey and time for some last-minute advice.

Jurgen started to talk to me after we ordered our food, "Andy, here it is, the day before you leave. Are you ready?"

"Well, I think I am. I have everything packed and I am aching to start racing."

"Have you called your parents?"

"Yes, I talked to them last night. They wish me well, but still questioned me about this trip. I don't get it; they act like I'm going to fail, like I shouldn't even try to do this because it's all a waste of time. Well, it's my time and I will waste it if I want to."

Jurgen looked a little sad. "I had hoped your parents would look more favorably once they saw your commitment over this winter, but it doesn't matter too much in the grand scope of things. You are the director sportif of your life and you choose what happens."

"I know, I just love to ride my bike, and it hurts that they don't support what I love."

"Let's look past this … Just remember the love for the bike. You need to be crazy for it, loathe it, and adore it. Don't let it take over your life, but let it mandate your priorities. You will get what you put into your bike. Keep your schedule consistent—no late nights at the disco. Enjoy your job and you will never work a day in your life. Enjoy the bike and the next year won't be a burden; it will be heaven for you. Do you understand me?"

"Yup! Have fun, enjoy it all, work hard, and I will get all I want."

"Andy, you've got it; it's all simple—life that is."

I wanted run to the airport and jump on a plane direct to Belgium. It was my time to conquer the world, but I had to wait one more night.

We all enjoyed the dinner and sat around talking for a long while after the main dinner was over. The waitress brought us our bill and three fortune cookies. Jurgen picked up the tray and put the tray in front of me. "Choose one."

I took mine and so did he and Amy. We each began to read out our fortunes. Jurgen's read, "The sum of all your problems will begin to present itself soon."

Jurgen laughed, "Problems: didn't know I had any; guess the sum of my problems is that I have none, and this is the way it was presented!"

Amy read out hers. "Two paths of reason will lead you to the same conclusion but different results than expected." She began to giggle with laughter.

"These are always too funny."

I opened my cookie up and read it to myself and stared.

I don't know how long I was motionless, but Amy brought me back to reality asking, "Well, dear, what's it say?"

I looked up from the fortune cookie, but my eyes still stayed on the paper between my fingers. "Um … well … it reads, 'You will make a name for yourself.'"

35

Jurgen shot me a perplexed glance. "Really? Nah ... let me see that."

I produced the little piece of paper to Jurgen and he read it. He then handed it to Amy and she looked surprised. Amy let out an exuberant giggle.

"Now isn't that peachy. Talk about a good sign. Couldn't ask for a better one."

I looked at her. "Yeah, but I didn't think it would be spelled out in black and white."

Jurgen looked to me. "Guess you gotta go now."

After that, Jurgen paid the bill and we got up to leave. As we approached the car, Amy grabbed Jurgen by the arm.

"Honey, aren't we forgetting something? You know, that thing?"

Jurgen looked affectionately over to Amy. "No, I haven't forgotten, Schatje. Guess we'll have to give it to him right now."

Jurgen walked over and unlocked the trunk, pulling out a set of wheels. "These are a little present for you journey. I knew you would need a good set of wheels while you pursue your cobblestone dreams, so I had Randy at the shop put together a nice set of tubbies for ya."

I gazed upon them: they were beautiful, and a masterpiece of art that even da Vinci would have been proud of producing. Each of the thirty-two three-crossed spokes sparkled under the streetlights' glow as the Mavic rim spun in my hands effortlessly on buttery smooth Dura-Ace hubs.

Jurgen began to talk as I stared in awe. "You know how meticulous Randy Sampson is, but with these wheels he took even more extra-special care. He ended up spending a whole day working on these wheels, putting in speed bearings, balancing it to perfection, making sure each spoke was tensioned just right. I even saw him re-glue the rear tire because it wasn't up to his standards. For him to go to those lengths, and not at my request, tells me you must have left a good impression on him this winter at the shop. These wheels are a compliment to you and your hard work. Use them well."

I looked at him. "Thank you, Jurgen. I will do these wheels justice."

"I know you will, Andy. Now let's go home and get some sleep; you will have a long day tomorrow."

III—Cobblestone Reality

My forehead pressed against the cold Plexiglas of the plane as I looked out the window while the earth began to disappear. The cars, the houses, the roads … all of it faded behind the obscurity of clouds. I was leaving my home, my friends, my family, the security of a uniform life for a far-off land, all in the pursuit of a dream. I couldn't tell if the knots in my stomach were from the ascent of the plane or the anticipation of what was to come. I knew nothing of life outside of the Northeast. How different could it all be?

I tried to sleep that night, but I couldn't. There was no use; too many thoughts ran through my head to give my mind the peace it needed for rest. I watched the in-flight movie for a little bit only to find my mind drifting back to the curiosity of what was to come once I stepped off the plane. I just sat there in my seat, looking out the window into the blackness of space. Out there lay a place, a place where I was going to fulfill my desires by my own accord and set myself upon the path of my choice. As the thought completed in my head and started to sink in, I tightened my cheek muscles and let a coy grin develop. I felt the hairs on the back of my neck rise in anticipation of what was to come.

"Sir …? Sir, would you like some coffee?"

I heard the voice, but it took me a couple of seconds to realize what was going on. I slurred out, "Uh … what … coffee, yeah, coffee would be nice."

I raised the coffee cup to my nose and drew in a full whiff of the sweet aroma. I let it awaken my brain and bring me to full attention. I was groggy and a bit stiff from sleeping weird. I glanced at my watch and noticed I only fell asleep for a few hours; it was two in the morning back home, but I was less than an hour from the Brussels airport.

I ended up just poking at my breakfast; I was too nervous to eat anything at the moment. I browsed through the airline magazine and killed a little time before we landed. The last thirty minutes, as we started our descent, seemed to be thirty hours. I just wanted the plane to land so I could end the anticipation.

As the plane broke through the clouds, I looked out my window to the lush, green fields below laced sporadically with brown and beige houses packed tightly together in rows along the streets. There seemed to be no pattern to it all, only roads from one cluster to another random cluster. I could see little dots moving on the roads. I wanted to reach down and just touch it all, to make it all feel real. I was so close to Europe!

The long-awaited "ding" of the seatbelt sign rang not only in the cabin, but also in my head, signaling my arrival. I conceived a contemplation: "The journey begins …"

I stepped off the plane onto the entrance ramp to the terminal. Crossing from one threshold to the next, I felt the cold, brisk air of a foreign land run along my skin. The reality was now real and tangible. Europe was under my feet. I walked through the long terminal and made my way to passport control. I waited in line and greeted the agent.

"Good morning."

In a solemn dictation he replied, "Passport and ticket."

I handed him both and waited while he stared emotionlessly at a computer screen.

"Reason for your visit?"

I exuberantly let out, "I am here to race my bike."

Looking up at my boyish face, his tone changed to a friendlier version of authoritative, but still he intoned abruptly, "Really? Well, you are in the right country. I hope you enjoy your visit."

"Thanks! I am sure I will."

I meandered along, following the baggage-claim symbols leading endlessly down halls and stairs to a row of screens. I looked for my flight and found my baggage carousel to be eight. I walked over and waited nervously for my bike and bag to arrive. I remember all the horror stories from guys who flew frequently about how badly airlines treated bikes. How bad would it be if I came all this way only to have my bike destroyed before I had the chance to ride it?

Just as I began to worry, I saw a uniform-clad kid jauntily rolling along with a baggage cart and a large bike box. He coasted to within ten feet then planted a foot down to come to a stop not ten inches from my feet.

"Is dit uw fiets?"

"Uh, yeah … and it's all there, thanks?"

"Geen problem."

He handed me the box. *"Alstublieft."*

I looked it over and the box was intact, with no signs of abuse. I collected my bag from the conveyor belt and made my way to the exit.

Jurgen told me I was going to need to take the train to Gent from the airport and meet Peter at the St. Peters station. That made it easy to remember, Peter at St. Peters. As I exited from customs control, I looked around to see people everywhere and looked for the train sign. I found a sign, started to follow, and I was led to a set of escalators and an arrow pointing down. I looked at my luggage cart and bike box; they weren't going down that way. I looked around for a bit and finally found an escalator.

Once at the level of the train station, I walked up to the ticketing office. With voracity in my voice I asked, "One ticket to Gent, please."

"One way or round trip?"

"One way"

"Eight euros forty cents."

I handed him the money and he pointed to platform two and the escalator. "It leaves in ten minutes."

I walked over, looked around, but saw no elevator. Guess I got to do it the hard way. I lugged the bike box and bag down the escalator and found a conductor.

"Hi, how ya doing? Where can I put this?"

"Hello, I can take it to the luggage compartment. Where is your stop?"

"Gent."

"Okay, you will need to find me once we get there to make sure the train doesn't take off with it still onboard."

"Oh, okay, will it be safe?"

"Yes."

"Are you sure?"

"I am quite sure."

"Okay, sorry, I am just nervous with my bike."

I watched him put the bike on the train and I hopped onboard and found a seat to myself.

As the train emerged from the dark tunnel and made its way out of Brussels, I looked out the window to gray skies and lush fields of green. I was in Belgium, land where bicycle racing was everywhere. I glanced up at the gentleman across the way reading the newspaper. I couldn't believe it: there was a full-color picture of a professional rider taking up half the front page. I looked a little closer and could tell the article was for a race, Kuurne-Bruxelles-Kuurne, taking place today. I could already tell this was going to be an epic experience.

As the train came to a halt in Gent, I quickly got off the train and ran over to the car carrying my bike. Sure enough the same attendant was there waiting to hand me my bike. "See, I told you I would have it ready. Good luck with your racing."

"Thanks, you have a great day."

I pulled my bike off the train, and from behind me I heard a raucous voice say, "You must be Andy Bennet."

I turned around to view a man in his early fifties wearing a cycling cap.

"I'm Peter Ververken, the friend of Jurgen Van Roy. Do you need some help with your bags?"

"Uh, sure, that would be great."

"Okay, my car is over this way."

We loaded up the bags in the car and we were off.

I looked over at Peter. His large nose was the focal feature of his weathered face. Dark brown hair and a burly build to his large frame helped carry his age well.

Peter spoke, "I am going to drop you off at the apartment first, let you unpack and get situated, then I will pick you up in the evening so you can have dinner at my house. We can talk about the season of racing over dinner. Do you have any questions?"

"Just one: when is the first bike race?"

"You can race next weekend, but give yourself some time to adjust to the time change. Oh, that reminds me; try to stay awake as long as you can tonight, until nine o'clock if you can, then go to sleep. It will help with the adjustment."

As his answer finished, we pulled up to the front of a bar. The small sign above the door read, "t'Kleintje."

"You will be living here above the bar with three other guys: another American, whom you will room with, a New Zealander, and a Russian. There are only two bedrooms, but a nice living room and a small kitchen. There is a small garage in the back where you can keep your bike. Let's get you moved in."

I walked up the stairs, following Peter up the side to the rear of the building. Entering the apartment gave way to the open kitchen and living room divided by a short serving bar. Past the living room there were two doors leading into the bedrooms and a bathroom separating each room. The apartment wasn't much to look at; it was raggedly furnished and there wasn't much lighting, but I didn't care. It could have looked like a prison and I would have been happy. All I wanted to do was ride my bike and show everyone what I was made of. I was itching to race, but I had to wait.

Peter looked around and said, "Guess the guys are out training. They should be back sometime soon. If you need something to eat in the meantime, there is a bakery just down the street to the left, along with a butcher. The grocery store is to the right. You can also get stuff to drink downstairs." Peter then started to pat his large belly and let out a deep chuckle. "Then again, it isn't the best stuff for ya. I'll be back around five o'clock tonight to pick you up, okay?"

"Sounds great. I will be ready then."

"Okay, let's go to the garage and put your bike away."

Peter then showed me the little garage and he was on his way.

I walked back inside the apartment and looked around. It wasn't being kept up in the best of conditions. There were a couple of dirty dishes here and there, some personal belongings strewn across the living room, but in all it was one of the cleaner cycling homes I had visited. I walked over to my room and looked around. It was probably twelve feet by sixteen feet, and there was a large window that looked out onto the street. I made my bed and began to unpack my things into an empty dresser. I was in the midst of placing a set of shorts into a drawer when I heard a ruckus from the living room.

I heard an accented English patois say, "Come on, Sergei, what else do you know?"

"Real niggaz don't die 'cause they eventually multiply."

41

"Damn, that is some funny shit. I don't think I will ever get tired of it."

As he finished the sentence, all three of the guys looked up at me and took account of me.

The same guy who was talking to Sergei said, "You must be Andy. The boss said you would be arriving today. Well, here are the introductions. I'm Ken O'Mally. Yeah, I know, it sounds Irish, but I'm not. I'm actually a Kiwi."

Pointing over to the altitudinous Sergei, "This here is Sergei Tolstov from Russia, and as you will soon find out, most of his English is limited to anything found on a rap album, especially the old-school stuff. And finally over here we have Troy Sanders, a fellow Yankee from the States. He will be rooming with you. You need the tour?"

"Uh, not really. Peter already showed me most all of it."

"Okay, well if you have any questions just ask."

Turning to the Sergei and Troy he said, "I don't know about you guys but I'm not going to stand here and start a mushroom factory. I'm going to go and get changed."

Everyone went about their ways and I returned to finish unpacking the rest of my clothes and my bike.

Returning from unpacking my bike I found Troy and Sergei in the living room watching TV and Ken in the kitchen.

Ken yelled out to me, "Hey Andy, you drink coffee?"

I riposted back, "I'd have an IV hooked up to me if I didn't have a fear of needles"

"Sounds like ya'll fit in just fine, mate. I am brewing up a fresh pot right now. Should be ready in a couple of minutes."

"Great, 'cause it's like five in the morning to me."

I went over to the couch and plopped lazily into the seat. I was tired and the jet lag was getting to me. I looked over to the TV to see Kuurne-Bruxelles-Kuurne on TV. Already it was day one and there was cycling on TV, LIVE! I looked over to Troy and asked, "Do they show all the races on TV?"

"I really don't know. Like you, I only just arrived."

Troy turned behind him and yelled over the back of the tatty couch, "Hey Ken, how many of the races are on TV a year here?"

Ken replied back across the room, "All the World Cups, the Grande Tours, and a handful of larger Belgian races like this one ... Andy, cream or sugar?"

"Uh, a little of both. Thanks."

Troy looked over to me, "Ken was here last year; he really knows the score better than either myself or Sergei ... Andy, you look familiar. Where are you from?"

"I grew up in Pennsylvania but I have been living in Boone, North Carolina, the last two years."

"Really? I am sure I raced against you a couple of times last year on the East Coast."

He paused a moment and began to circularly rub a finger on his temple, as if manually rewinding his brain.

"Hey, you were the guy who flatted on the final day of Fitchburg. Yeah, I remember, you were going well, but then in the final corner ... One of my teammates was in the break with you. He said you were like a man possessed that day."

"Possessed?"

I looked over to see Ken standing with a cup of coffee.

"Sounds like ya got the right mindset for here; you need to be slightly certifiably crazy to do this sport."

Tilting his coffee cup at the screen he said, "That right there is some downright hard racing."

My new roommates and I lay back and relaxed watching the TV. After about thirty minutes of the race, I began to notice something: there were no commercials. I just couldn't figure it out so I asked the man with all the answers.

"Ken, where are the commercials?"

"Commercials? You won't find any during this or any other major sporting event. Belgians just don't like to have their sports events interrupted; it's supposed to take away from the grandeur of the event."

I couldn't believe it, no commercials. I guess in the end it was a trade-off, because back home I would be delighted with Liggetisms and here I had to settle for a language that I could not understand.

The race still had forty kilometers to go and I had a rumble in my stomach. I hadn't had anything to eat since early in the morning, but with all the excitement of my new surroundings I hadn't noticed.

I decided to go down to the local bakery and get a little something to eat.

Exiting to the left from the alley, I began to observe more of the street around me. Buildings of the gray and brown persuasion fitted tightly one next to each other, with the front of each coming all the way to the sidewalk, no front lawns. I walked no more than three hundred feet and arrived at the bakery. I expected to find some store all by itself, but instead it was nestled in between the other houses along the street, integrated into its surroundings. I went to pull open the door but it wouldn't budge. I looked inside to see people, so I tried again, and it wouldn't open. Just then a person on the inside pulled the door open. He looked fairly amused and I was a bit embarrassed. "I guess you gotta push doors open around here."

He and the young lady behind the counter cracked a smile. The bakery was small, maybe just thirty feet wide and twelve feet deep, with one door in and one door out. Small as it was, the back wall was filled with racks of assorted breads, and the case in front of me was teeming with delectable-looking treats. Once the lady finished with the man, she looked over to me.

"Hi, do you speak English?"

"Yes, a little bit."

"Okay, well, what is good?"

She snickered a little laugh. "Everything, but you might like the *Chocoladekoeken*."

She pointed to a small, fluffy pastry with chocolate melted on the top.

"They are filled with a little chocolate, and have some spread on top."

This place was going to be one of evil temptation, filled with so many choices on how to make a rider fat. I finally asked for two of them and grabbed a bottle of chocolate milk-looking drink out of a drink cooler. I paid and started to walk back to the apartment.

Back at the apartment I watched Kuurne-Bruxelles-Kuurne end in a beautifully timed solo attack from a small group in the final kilometers. It was done with the precision of a skilled tactician. I was watching the winner being interviewed as the image slowly faded while the muffled sounds around me turned to silence.

I heard a distant voice saying to me, "Andy, you need to get up. It's not good to dose off for too long your first day."

I looked up to see a blurry vision of Ken in front of me, giving my foot a bit of a shake. "Huh ... was I asleep?"

"Yeah, mate, but not too long. Sorry to wake ya up, but it will help to stay awake. Trust me."

I nodded and rubbed some saliva dripping down the side of my chin. Man, was I tired. I looked around for a clock: 3:30. Still had some time to kill before Peter would be here. I decided to take a walk around the block to loosen up the legs and explore my new home.

Coming out of the alley, I decided to go right in lieu of my previous choice of left. The city was utterly amazing. All the buildings were pressed right up against each other, almost making one solid building, but of varying heights and colors. I walked for a few blocks and turned right. After I turned the corner I stopped and stared. I must have stood there for at least thirty seconds, just looking. Cobbles. The whole road was lined with large, gray cobbles. I bent down and made a long, slow examination of the smooth, rounded surface. There were many a cold days I had dreamed of seeing cobbles ... real ... tangible. I listened to Jurgen, Frank, and others talk about the races in Europe, and always these little round stones were regarded with a mixture of admiration and trepidation. These stones were what helped build the legends of cycling.

I ran my finger over the surface; it was cold and smooth. Smoothed from years, maybe even centuries, of wear, but yet it was still there, enduring time. I got up and looked the street up and down. The reality of it all hit me ... Europe, Belgium, Gent. I had arrived! I walked lazily back to the apartment, successfully killing most all of the time before Peter was to arrive. I hopped into the bathroom for a quick shower to wake myself up and freshen up from the long trip.

* * *

Peter arrived at the apartment on time, a good sign for my part, as tardiness isn't something I like; in fact, I dreadfully hate being late. We piled into the small team station wagon and headed for his house. Peter lived not even ten minutes' drive by car, and maybe even that much by bike, because we hit a little bit of a traffic snag along the way. Upon getting out of the car I asked Peter, "About how big is Gent? Size that is."

"Oh, it's fairly big, about ten kilometers wide, one of the bigger cities in Belgium."

"Really, is that all? That isn't that big where I come from."

"True, you need to realize Belgium is quite small, so by our standards it's a really big city."

"I have to keep telling myself it's all a matter of perspective."

"That would be a good idea, in this matter and others to come. Let's get inside; it's a bit cold out here and I don't want you to catch a cold your first week here. Jurgen wouldn't be too pleased with me."

Peter's house was a nice, modest home situated on the outskirts of the city. It had its own small yard in the front and back, which he told me wasn't too common when living this close to the city. Inside I met his sweet wife, Celina. When I went to give her a customary handshake as a hello, she glared amusingly at me.

"Now ... Andy is it? Here in Belgium we typically will give each other a little cheek kiss to say hello ... You Americans and your handshakes."

"I'm sorry, I didn't know."

"That is okay. Better to make the mistake with me than some pretty Belgian girl later. Oh, it's one kiss informally and three formally, okay?"

"I think I'll remember."

I gave her three quick pecks on the cheek like I had seen in the movies, but never thought I would actually be one of those people giving cheek kisses in real life.

Jurgen started, "Would you like some coffee, Andy?"

"Yes please."

Celina replied, "Okay, I will bring some out soon."

Just as Celina was rounding the corner, a little girl came running from the same way and leaped onto Peter's leg.

"Papa!"

Peter looked down and picked her up.

"This here is Annika. She will be seven next month. Now, let's go into the living room and get comfortable."

Right as Peter and I sat down, Celina walked in with the coffee.

"So, Andy, what are your impressions so far with Gent?"

"Well, it's really nice. The people seem really friendly."

"And your roommates?"

"Ken is really helpful, Troy is nice, and Sergei didn't say much."

"Oh, Sergei, his English isn't good, but he can understand most of what you say to him. He is one strong rider from what I was told, and he looks it."

"So are there other Americans racing for the team?"

"Other than you and Troy, no. In fact, the team is all Belgian riders; you four above the t'Kleintje are the only foreign riders on the team."

"Oh, I thought there might be more."

"Nope, we are primarily a Belgian team. I let a few foreign riders each year join the team."

"So what races are we going to be doing this year?"

"You are going to start off racing *Kermesse* races in the beginning. I want to see how you can handle the race speeds and the flow of the race. Kermesse races are typically around 110- to 120-kilometers and average forty to forty-five kilometers per hour in speed, but do realize this is on a winding course, usually with a lot of corners. The racing style here is much more different than in the States. The best advice I can give you is stay toward the front. Once you show promise in the Kermesse racing, you can be selected for the larger, faster, and longer UCI events. The lowest ranking is classified a 1.12, and then it goes up to a 1.6. Both of these races can only have amateur riders in them, no professionals. The highest UCI that you are allowed to race as an *'elite zonder contract'* is a 1.5, which contains both professionals and amateurs. Of course, our team isn't one of the biggest ones in Belgium, so this class of race probably won't be done. For the BASE-Duvel Cycling Team, our biggest objectives are the prestigious Interclub races here in Belgium. There are ten races a year given the *'Topcompetitie'* distinction and hold a lot of prestige. These are the biggest races for amateurs here in Belgium. Do you follow it all?"

"Kinda. I guess I will figure it out in due time."

"I am sure you will. But for now you need to focus on the Kermesse races; they are hard, sometimes harder than the UCI races, so don't think they aren't important. In the apartment is a *Cyclink* magazine. Ask Ken to show you how to find the local races that you can attend. Everyone in the house is twenty-three and over, so you will all be doing the Elite Zonder Contract races and not the *Beloften*—or 'Espoir' as you call it back home—races."

"So what do you expect out of me?"

"I expect no less than one hundred percent of what you are capable of, and if you can give me 105 percent I will be even more pleased. This is your time, your money, and your energy."

"Well, I want to win a race … I want to win a European race!"

"That is ambitious, but we'll see how things go. Just take things one step at a time, Andy, and you will be fine."

"I will win a race. If I don't, this was all for nothing. I am here to prove foremost to myself that I can do this, and in the process to those who think I can't do it."

Peter broadened a wide smile. "Jurgen was right, there is a fire inside of you. We'll see what happens with some time."

Just then, Celina interrupted and let us know dinner was ready.

I was treated to a wonderful traditional Belgian dish of *Gentse Stoverij*; slow-cooked beef in a gravy base served with French fries, or *friets*. We talked a little bit more, but mostly it was about my last season of racing and what I did in the winter. I got the impression Peter liked me, and I trusted Jurgen to put me in good hands. I thanked Celina for dinner and departed with Peter for the apartment. When I reached my bed, it was only eight at night, and I fell asleep still in my clothes.

* * *

I opened heavy eyelids to a sky with no sign of light behind the veil of gray, and I arose to the aroma of coffee in the crisp morning air, which pulled me from my slumber to the kitchen. In there I found Ken preparing his cereal breakfast. I looked up to him.

"Good morning, Ken, is there any coffee left over?"

"Top o' the morning to ya, Andy. Sure there is coffee, and help yourself to some Muesli."

"Muesli? What is that?"

Ken chuckled. "Only the cheapest calorie-dense food in Belgium. It's a typical breakfast food here and comes in one-kilo bags for about one euro twenty-five. So really cheap!"

"Oh, I think I'll try it out, 'cause cheap sounds good to me."

"Yeah, tell me about it. I usually add a little yogurt to it to soften up the whole deal, but you can add milk if you like."

It looked liked crispy oats with some nuts and dried fruits in it. It had to be real healthy 'cause the one dry spoonful I tried didn't have much taste. Ken interjected, "They make some sweeter Muesli at the store, but it costs more. I will usually add a little of that to the regular stuff to give it a bit of a better taste. Tell you what; I need to go shopping today. How about you come with me, that way I can give you a breakdown of the local foods."

"Sounds great. Are you going for a ride today? 'Cause I wanna get out and see the city and area."

"I'll be going for about three hours. You're welcome to come along. I think I will hit up the canal road down the Schelde for some coffee and back. That is kinda the staple training route around here."

"Sounds like fun!"

I returned to my imitation horse-feed breakfast and enjoyed the smooth sensation of coffee flowing into my stomach.

After breakfast, I prepared myself for my ride. The temperature outside was slightly chilly, even for my Northeastern blood, and I piled on a couple of layers of clothes. Outside I met up with all of my roommates and Ken started us off on our ride. Roaming through the city on bike was awesome, and I was able to explore and see even more of the city than on my first day. The veil of tiredness lifted from my jet-lagged eyes as my legs started to bear down against the pedals and brought to full scope the city's beauty. I was most awestruck by the city's myriad historical buildings, many of which were older than the U.S. The city's sporadic setup of streets left my head spinning, and I was grateful to have a guide to navigate the winding and meandering roads.

As we rolled through the city we crossed various unmarked and raised intersections. The first time we came up to one of the four-way intersections I saw a car on the left side and yelled out, "Car left!" and started to brake for the car.

Behind me Troy and Sergei started to yell, "No, no, keep going. Don't stop!"

I quickly accelerated and we rolled through the intersection with the car waiting patiently for us to pass. Ken looked over to me.

"Here in Belgium, they have a lot more respect the cyclists than back in the States. That car had to give us the right of way; it was a yield to the right intersection. They will even yield most of the time to a cyclist when he is on the left. So don't freak out when there are cars near. No one here wants to hurt a cyclist."

I heard the words, but it went against the grain of what I knew to be true. I have had one too many hillbilly rednecks throw stuff at me or try to run me off the road to break my defensive habits. The way the cars waited and respected the people on a bike astonished me. Being able to ride along and not have to worry if the next car to pass you would loosen your last mortal coil was a relief to the senses.

We reached the outskirts of the city in about fifteen minutes, and the spacing of the houses became less and less with the distance. Before long, we were beside the Schelde Canal. The road veered onto a path with a circular sign of a bike on a blue background, and another sign after it with a car and a red slash through it. The road paralleling the canal was reserved just for cyclists and your occasional moped, which Ken explained was one of the most common modes of transportation here in Belgium because of the small distances to amenities and the high cost of a driver's license.

Once out on the canal, spring's standard sweet smell was in the air, glazed with a light pungent stench that permeated my nostrils. I pulled in another whiff of the air only to become inundated with a stronger and fouler version of the odor. I looked over at Troy to ask what it was, but he only shrugged.

Sergei then said to me, "There, da shit-truck!"

I looked to my right to see a large truck with a huge barrel on the back with two long hose attachments coming from the barrel. Ken looked back and laughed.

In a great French accent he said, "*Mon ami*, I give to you *Le Odeur de Flanders*: the smell of rural Belgium. A rustic blend of farm and animal combined in our special fragrance trucks to make not only the wonderful perfume, but it also doubles as a quality fertilizer." He pulled a large draw of air into his lungs. "Ahh, dis year seems to be especially pungent!"

We all were trying to hold our bikes upright as the hilarious impersonation by Ken caused all of us to laugh and veer from our prescribed path.

As it turns out, the large truck was really spewing shit. The farmers often concoct their own fertilizers on their land under huge tarps covered by tires. They let it all ferment for a year and then liquefy it for spreading the following season. As Ken put it, "It's not the worst smell in the world, but it's damn near close. But not to worry, as they generally only spray during the month of March, so the smell doesn't linger all year."

We continued our ride, trying to remember not to breathe from our noses. I started to talk to Troy and he was telling me that this ride he had already done two times. The Schelde was a long canal from Gent to Oudenaarde and beyond that was frequented by many cyclists because of its length and extremely sparse traffic. There is a nice little café down the way where everyone would usually stop for a nice coffee on easy days.

The rest of the ride wasn't too bad. We ended up going to the right in Oudenaarde and heading out toward some of the climbs in the direction of Geraardsbergen. Troy was telling me the roads were part of the Tour of Flanders route, but all I could do was look down at the names still painted down on the road. How many names were there? I could read names like Museeuw, Vandenbroucke, Mattan, Van Peteghem, and Bettini. The names I had seen countless times watching the spring classics on TV and they were under my own tires! We crested the hill and started a winding descent down a road between two farms. I was on the roads of the Tour of Flanders and I started dreaming of the day when my name to would be painted on the roads of Flanders.

The rest of the ride went smoothly. We ticked off just over three and half hours on the bike and it felt good to finally get the legs moving after all the travel. My form was definitely off a little from the jet lag, but I wasn't feeling too bad. Our timing couldn't have been any better, because no less than ten minutes after we got home from our ride I heard a resonating repetition on the roof and peered outside. Rain. Ken looked at me over by the door.

"Andy, welcome to Belgium, where the weather is just about as unpredictable as the racing; well, almost."

I laughed and returned to my room to change and grab a quick shower.

After I dressed I found Ken in the living room writing stuff down.

"Man, I am hungry. I really need to eat something before we go to the store. If I don't I'm likely to buy them out of food."

"Well, I got some apples in the cabinet. You're welcome to one."

"Thanks!"

I grabbed an apple and headed out the door with Ken and a backpack. In the garage I started to grab my racing bike and Ken cut me off.

"Andy, don't take your racing bike; take one of these," he said, pointing to some decrepit-looking bikes in the corner of the dark shed. I shot him a stare that said, "You're kidding." He looked back at me.

"These are what we call '*stadsfiets*,' or city bikes. Everyone around here uses them for transportation and we don't need to worry about these getting stolen near as much as a nice racing bike. Anyways, your racing bike will suffer enough this year. That I guarantee."

He grabbed the saddle of the closest stadsfiets and rolled it my way.

We rolled out of the alleyway and hung a right. Ken explained we were going to the Delhaize, a large, chain-style supermarket. It was there you could find most everything you wanted to buy, but he warned me about getting breads, meats, and vegetables.

"Here in Belgium you really don't need to buy those things for the week like you Yanks do back home. There is a great butcher around the corner from the house, and the fruit stand and bakery carry only fresh stock. You can pay a few cents more and get way better quality."

The Delhaize ended up being far away by Belgian standards, a ten-minute leisurely bike ride. The shopping was nice. The store reminded me of the States, except the fact that everything was in a foreign language. Well, really two: Dutch and French. I never realized how much you could deduce from pictures till that day. If I didn't see a picture on the label, I wasn't going to buy it. My next trip was going to include a Dutch-English dictionary.

The whole shopping time ended up being just over an hour, more than I had ever spent shopping for food. I prefer the Navy Seal—style in-and-out for my shopping experience. I waited in line, and Ken pulled up behind me with his cart.

I started to place some cans of what I hoped to be Mexican-style refried beans when Ken said with a grin on his face, "You're about to experience the most stressful part of life here in Belgium."

I looked at him queerly and continued to put my groceries on the conveyor belt. Soon it was my turn, and the young girl behind the counter said, "Hallo," and something else way to fast for me to even understand the sounds of, much less the meaning.

I looked at her blankly and muttered out, "Umm, do you speak English?"

"Do you have a Delhaize card?"

"Oh … uh … no."

She grabbed a plastic bag, sat it on the counter, and started to quickly scan the items on the belt. I just stood there waiting, and then after about minute I looked over at the end of the counter. There wasn't a sacker; my groceries were just sitting there. Then I looked over to Ken, who had that same smirk on his face, and I realized what he had meant.

I grabbed my backpack and started to shove my groceries in there as fast as I could, but as fast as I went, the cashier lady was even faster. I just couldn't keep up. In the middle of me still bagging the remainder of my groceries, she looked over to me and said, "Sixty-three euros and fifty-four cents, please."

I fumbled around with my wallet and still tried to bag the rest of the groceries. The whole time, Ken stood there watching the whole debacle with much amusement. Eventually I shoved all the groceries into my backpack and watched Ken, who had organized his groceries so they would bag faster, go through the whole process without much problem.

On the way out he said, "Sorry to do that to ya, but it's kinda something everyone's gotta go through. The Belgians are really laidback, but for some reason the grocery counter is the one time they try to speed things up. Of course, you did better than Troy. He didn't realize what was going on till the girl had finished scanning everything."

"Well, you did give me a warning … well, kinda."

"Now you know, so it won't be as bad next time."

We started on our way back to the apartment and stopped by the local butcher. Ken led the way, and upon entering, I heard a gentleman behind the counter let out a loud statement.

"Ah, Ken. How are you today?"

"Fritz, alles goed met mij, en met jou?"

"Het is fijn. So who is your friend?"

"Fritz, this is Andy Bennet, an American. He is going to live with us over at the apartment this year."

"Ah, Andy—good to meet you. Welcome to Belgium."

I grinned and replied, "Thanks, it's been really cool so far."

"Well, I will make sure you have some good meat. A nice steak and you will be strong for many kilometers."

I laughed a little at the exuberance of Fritz; he was so friendly and I had known him for all of two minutes. Ken motioned to the beef.

"I'll take 500 grams of the beef and then two chicken breasts."

"*En wat had u gewenst?*"

"The beef."

Fritz looked at him and interjected, "*In het Nederlands Alstublieft.*"

Ken smiled. "*Oh ja—oke … Ik zou graag vijfhounderd gram biefstuk hebben en twee kippeborsten.*"

"*Is dat alles?*"

"*Ja dat is alles.*" Ken motioned to me.

"Uh, do I have to say it in Dutch?"

Ken and Fritz started to laugh. Ken said to me, "Nah, I just make Fritz here force me to practice my Dutch when I order; helps me learn. You can order in English."

I was glad, 'cause if I needed to order in Dutch I was going to have to become a vegetarian, and not by choice.

The bakery was just about the same way. Ken knew the lady and her husband, Kathleen and Stephan, who were very friendly. It was cool to walk into a store and have people address you by name and then ask how you were doing. They wanted to know how Ken was doing, how his riding was going, just normal friendly conversation. They asked me where I was from, why I came to Belgium, and asked me questions about America.

I left the bakery with the feeling that the people at the bakery and butcher were not just there out of necessity, but that they enjoyed their jobs and liked being there. Ken continued with the orientation.

"Around the corner and to the left is another bakery, and then three buildings down from there is another butcher. They are the backup bakery and butcher which you can use when either of these is closed on their day off, which is Tuesdays for the bakery and Thursday for the butcher."

Back at the apartment, I joined everyone in a little bit of group collusion as we made a large dinner and shared the workload. I was put on pasta sauce and noodle duty while Troy prepared a salad and Ken and Sergei cooked up some meat to go with the meal. As it turns out Sergei was a really good cook, and Ken knew how to fend well for himself, but Troy wasn't that well domesticated for kitchen duty. He was young like the rest of us, but had never lived on his own, staying at home till this year.

Over dinner, we shared stories of our cycling exploits and about our hometowns. Every once in a while we had some miscommunications, either unknown Queen's English words used by Ken, or Sergei's limited vocabulary. It was nice, however, to finally begin to bond with my roommates. After we cleaned up dinner, Ken clapped his hands together loudly.

"Mates, it's time to learn the best part of our locale here in Gent. We are living above a wonderful café, t'Kleintje, and it is all of seventy steps to get to the bar. I know! I had to crawl it last year."

With that, I ran into my room to grab my wallet and followed everyone down to the bar.

Walking into t'Kleintje, I was hit with a thick layer of smoky glaze against my eyes. The dim light took a minute for my eyes to adjust to, and the room came into focus despite a faint haze of smoke. Darkly stained woodwork against deep foliage green ingrained itself along much of the bar as the pungent smell of burnt tobacco and stale hops permeated my nostrils. As we walked in people paused to take notice for a moment then went about their activities. I surveyed the room: lots of older men smoking and talking loudly with both with their voices and hands, but there were a few families enjoying some light dinners and snacks. A TV played in the background with a soccer game, which drew most of the attention of the men at the bar.

Ken walked over to the bar to an older gentleman and said, "Bijorn, how are you this evening?"

"Ken, I am fine. So who do we have here?"

"Everyone, this is Bijorn De Smet, he is the owner of the bar and a sponsor of the team. Bijorn, this here is Troy Sanders and Andy Bennet, both from America. And here we have Sergei Tolstov from Russia."

Bijorn smiled at each of us and asked, "And who here will get us the first win of the season?"

Everyone looked around at each other, but no one wanted to speak. I certainly wasn't prepared to make quite so grandiose a statement. Bijorn went on.

"Well, what do you think, Ken? You going to win again this year?"

"I'll try now. Can't guarantee anything in this sport, ya know."

"True, true, well, how about a round on the house … to toast the season. I think some Duvels would be appropriate."

Bijorn was a curious-looking guy. In his early sixties with plump, rosy cheeks, he had short, gray hair with small wisps of brown hair clinging his youth to him. He was a short gentleman with a large potbelly that rounded out his pear shape, which he amplified by his short steps that made him gently wobble side to side when he walked. A small mustache covered and minimized even further his small lips, even when he talked, which left me slightly bewildered.

While Bijorn was preparing the drinks, I walked over to the wall next to the bar. It was there I saw photos, lots of photos, of cyclists, some in black-and-white, but most in color. I continued to look at the wall and came across a photo labeled "Oosterzele—Ken O'Malley." There was Ken in front of a crowd of people, holding a bouquet of flowers. This must have been the win that Bijorn was talking about. I wondered why Ken had never mentioned winning a race.

I continued to look at the photos, but then I felt a tap on my shoulder. I turned around to see the thin smile of Bijorn with a glass of Duvel held toward me.

"*Alstublieft.*"

I accepted the glass and he stepped up beside me.

"He looks much younger there."

I looked over at Bijorn in bewilderment.

"Who does?"

Pointing to the young rider in the photo, he said, "Jurgen, of course. Don't you see the resemblance?"

I stared a little more at the photo right in front of me and I could see it in the eyes, but he had such a glow of youth in that photo.

"This was taken in Jurgen's first year as a pro. He was such an aggressive rider, the older riders of the peloton use to complain about him making the races too hard; but that was just because he would plan his attacks at the moment he knew the top riders to be hurting. He was a brilliant rider at timing."

You could hear tones of respect overlaid with reverence in his voice; it carried the words with no effort.

"How did you know I know Jurgen?"

"Oh, Peter Verveken, of course. You will find that cycling is a small community here, very close. Now, let's go and toast to the season before the beer runs flat."

We all raised our glasses and Bijorn led the toast. The first round went by quickly; another round showed up to our surprise at the end of the first. By the end of the third round, I was beginning to feel really tipsy. Bijorn regaled us with stories of some of the greats of Belgian cycling: Merckx, Museeuw, Van Looy, De Vlaeminck, Maertens, and Van Steenbergen. It was Ken who finally reminded us of the time and that we needed some sleep. I went for my wallet, but Bijorn told me to put it back. Tonight was his treat.

So we all walked back up to the apartment and quickly dispersed to our bedrooms. I was asleep within two minutes of my head hitting my pillow.

IV—Baptism by Fire

The rest of the week was spent roaming around the numerous roads of Flanders. Not a single one of the roads seemed go in a particular direction for any amount of time. Just when I thought I would be going north toward Holland I was heading to the west toward the coast. After the third day, I threw out my embedded logic for road navigation and used a tip Jurgen had told me before I left: use the towns, not the roads.

The funniest of all the directional conundrums was a sign reading *"Andere Richting."* This sign was grouped with and similar to the directional city signs I always saw around. So I decided one day to follow the signs to the town. I spent over three hours that day following the signs, but I couldn't find the town Andere Richting, so I gave up and headed home.

Back at the apartment, I pulled out my map again to find the town, but to no avail. Finally, I went and asked Ken. No sooner had the words "Andere Richting" rolled off my tongue than he started to laugh hysterically, and it took him a good minute to gain his composure.

"What is so funny? I spent all day looking and I couldn't find the town, but I saw the signs all over Flanders."

Still trying to gain full composure he blurted out, "Andy, do you know what 'Andere Richting' means?"

"Uh—no."

"It's Dutch for 'Other Direction.' When you get to a town's center and there are signs, you have a sign for say Alter, then Andere Richting. So you can go to either Alter or the 'other direction.' It's how the Belgians navigate. So if it is not direction Alter, it's the other way!"

I looked at him blankly: it made no sense, but neither did the road structure in Belgium. No four rights make a square, so why was anything else going to work out logically? I had always prided myself on being able to find my way well, but I was a bit embarrassed that day.

Ken then laid down the map and settled his index finger down to the south of Gent.

"There, Oudenaarde; that is where the Kermesse will be on Saturday. I did the race last year; it's a big one and there will be plenty of riders there. It's only thirty or so kilometers away, so we will ride there, but Peter and a soigneur will be there to feed and support us."

I gazed down at the map and elongated a smirking grin on my face as I felt the excitement start to churn in my stomach. It had been a while since my last race, and that itch had grown to a burn that needed to be tempered. I leaned in a little more.

"So what can I expect at this race?"

Ken brazenly said, "Expect …? Expect to learn how it all happens here in Belgium. This is an old race and there is a lot of pride in winning it."

I coyly interjected, "So it would be good if I win the race?"

"Ha! If you win the race I will give you my bike."

"Yeah, yeah … I got ya, so how long will it be?"

"Well, for the answer to this and about every question you have for any race happening in Belgium, you will need to consult the good book, and not the Bible, but the *CycLink*. It is a bi-monthly publication by the Belgian Cycling Federation that lists all the races of Belgium. Seeing as we are all over twenty-two, we can't do the Beloften but will do the Elite Zonder Contract. An elite rider without contract."

Pointing to the name of the town, he said, "Just to the right of every town you will find an abbreviation. Here we have an 'OV' for Oost-Vlaanderen, which is where we live. Below that is the total distance; in this case, one hundred and sixteen kilometers, and then the number of laps and their distance. Here eleven laps of ten and a half kilometers. The next line is the race's payout. Standard payout for every race in Belgium is 620 euros, thirty places deep. But for this race they will be giving out an extra five euros for places thirty-one to forty. After that you have the location of the *inschrijving*, or registration, followed on the next line by the start times. On the final line you have where the *kleedkamers*, or changing rooms, are located." Ken grasped the magazine firmly in his hands and started off in the first lecturing tone I had heard all week. "Now, don't you lose this. It stays here on the kitchen counter by the phone. The *CycLink* goes nowhere else."

I nodded my head in acceptance and started to walk to my room. I lay down on my bed and propped my legs up against the wall. I began to rub out the lactic acid and work through a small knot that had formed on my left hamstring from the day's riding. I started to let my mind drift and began to imagine the race. Oudenaarde. It was to be the place of my baptism by fire into the world of European racing in two day's time. I had endured through a hard East Coast winter and left my family, my life, my securities, and stepped firmly outside of my boundaries of comfort, all for a dream. The fountainhead of the trip had only just allowed me to feel the path below my feet. I have been taken blindfolded and placed on an unknown road minutes before dusk. Upon lifting the blindfold, I can see the outline of my road, but not its true form. The commencement of my dream begins with the sun cresting the horizon when the break of first light will reveal the path I have chosen. Clarity of reality will become known. Saturday is the day.

* * *

I arose Saturday with grin on my face. I pulled in a large whiff of air through my nostrils and exhaled deeply from my mouth. I leaped to my feet, grasped my hands together, and stretched them to the ceiling, prompting my rigid body into awakening from its rest.

I walked into the kitchen and poured myself a large bowl of Muesli. It was between my second and third spoonfuls of the oat-grain concoction that I paused and listened to the gentle, repetitious rattle against the panes of glass. My head turned to the window above the sink. Droplets of water clung to the window in suspension. The sight brought forth a thought that dwelled in my brain: today's race was going to be a more literal baptism into European racing than anticipated.

Troy and Sergei walked into the room, noticed my stare toward the window, and in synchronization both their mouths gravitated southward into frowns. Sergei let out in a deep, short breath.

"Belgium and rain, always!"

Troy responded in similar fashion.

"Why today? It's been fine all week."

I snapped a quick rebuttal.

"It's Murphy's Law: if something can go wrong, it will go wrong. Just have to roll with the punches and play the hand you're dealt. We can't control the dealer, but we can control how we use the cards we got."

Troy looked a little more pleased, but Sergei was still muttering something in Russian, more than likely derogatory about the weather. I continued to finish off my breakfast and started to think about the race.

After breakfast I went to my room to prepare my clothing and make sure I was prepared for the race. I laid out all my clothes, my shoes, my helmet, checked through my mental list of pre-race preparation, and finished quickly. It was only 9:30 in the morning and I still had five and a half hours till the race. It was strange to have so much free time before a race. The whole summer was filled with races that started either very early in the morning for a road race or late in the evening for a criterium. It was going to take some adjusting to get used to this new timetable.

I then headed over to the living room, where I found Ken relaxing on the couch. I sat down next to him and started up a little conversation.

"So, anything too different I need to remember for the race?"

"Safety pins. You got any?"

"Safety pins, why would I need those?"

"'Cause not one of the races provides you with them, almost every Yank that comes over forgets them. There is a small jar with some extras over on the kitchen counter if you need some. Other than that, not much else other than standard race supplies."

I turned my attention and watched TV to kill most of the time before we left. It was just a conscious distraction, because in truth my subconscious was still on the race. Questions kept running though my head. Could people here be as strong as the brave souls who returned to tell tales of the infamous Belgian Kermesse? I knew I had prepared for this season well; in fact, I had prepared immaculately, but I still had yet to really ride at my limits against other riders, so I had no comparison for my current form.

It was about 1:15 when we headed out. Rain quickly soaked through my clothing, though my chest stayed dry because of my rain cape. We rolled though the streets of Gent carefully through a cluster of cars and bikes, which in spite of the rain seemed unfazed by the wetness.

We made it to the canal road along the Schelde and it was virtually, albeit by Belgian standards, a straight shot to the race.

Once we hit the outskirts of Oudenaarde, Ken navigated us through the maze of roads toward the race. Once he found his bearings, he looked back.

"Now, when you are looking for a race, there are two important things to know. One, where is the church, 'cause that is the center of town where the race will more than likely be. Second are these signs," he said, pointing to a small, round, blue sign with a red border and a slash through it. Below was a small arrow pointing upwards. "These are the no-parking signs. This means we are on the course; well, more likely than not on the course."

Sure enough, after a few turns I started to see barriers along the side of the road. Ahead I could see a cluster of people, cars, riders, and vending stands.

Ken stated, "Up here is the start of the race. Inscription is in the café on the left-hand side and on the right is the finishing stand. We need to inscribe first then find Peter to have a place to stash our stuff. If we can't find him we can put our things at the soccer field down the road; the changing rooms are there."

We still had three-fourths of an hour left till the race, so time to spare.

I followed Ken's lead and placed my bike at the side of the café. Outside there were riders, but more people than I expected. We weren't in that large of a town, but there was a mass of people here for the race, even with the dire weather. Entering the café, I felt as if I was in a dense fog, but this fog burned my lungs. The haze of smoke made me let out a little cough, and the darkness left my eyes adjusting for a couple of seconds. There was a packed plethora of people in the bar, and I had to bump and push my way through them to follow Ken.

Once we were more to the back of the bar, I saw the line for registration. I waited there and observed the room. It was filled with people drinking, smoking, chatting away, and enjoying a Saturday afternoon. Just as I finished surveying the room I heard a voice directed in my direction. I heard it again from my left and looked over to see an old guy asking me something in Flemish. I smiled and just stood there not knowing what to do. I didn't know this guy. Again he asked me the same thing.

I finally said to him, "Sorry, I don't speak Flemish."

"Oh, you speak English. Ahh, an Englishman?"

"Nope, I'm an American."

A look of surprise bloomed from his face.

"An American … really …? Why did you come all this way?"

"Why else but to race bikes?"

"Well, you have come to the right place. There are plenty of races here in Belgium and many fast racers. So, you win the race today?"

"Uh, I'll try."

"You a strong racer?"

"I think I am."

"Okay, I think I will bet on you." The old man then firmly gripped my arm. "You look strong … a strong American racer … you will do well."

I was a little more than freaked out at this point, but I kept my cool despite being groped by an old Belgian guy. Troy, who was standing behind me, was about to bust out of his skin in laughter at my peril.

The line moved forward and I finally arrived at the registration table. I followed the lead of Ken by first giving my license to the first official. He took a good long look at it, flipped it over to my photo, then back again. He said to the official next to him, "Bennet, Andy, van Amerika, BASE-Duvel. …" The second official looked up after writing down all the information, pointed to a spot next to my license number, and held out a pen in his other hand. I signed my name and kept moving forward. The next guy had a small tobacco box with coin and cash. He said something to me in Flemish, which I guessed was the cost of the race, and I handed him a ten-euro note. I knew it would cover the cost of the race, and sure enough I got two euros back. The final official typed away on an old-fashioned swing-arm typewriter. After he was done, he handed back my license with the customary *"Alstublieft."* The whole process took no more than thirty seconds. No fuss, no muss.

Outside I waited for Troy and Sergei to get out of the line.

I leaned over toward Ken and asked, "What did that old guy mean by he was betting on me?"

"Exactly what he said; he was going to bet on you." Pointing over to a large, black chalkboard, he said, "At a lot of the races there are bookies who will take bets on any of the racers. You will have your number and then last name followed by two numbers. The first is the multiplier payout for a win and the second is the multiplier for a top three."

"Wow, so we're kinda like horse racing for Belgium?"

"Sorta like horse racing, but it's mostly to add some excitement to the race. This is a social event for most of these people, not just a bike race. When summer rolls around, the Kermesse races will be just a small part of the Kermis, or carnivals, each town has every year."

The intricate way the race revolved around the town and the fact people actually wanted a race to come to their town amazed me.

Troy and Sergei made their way out of the bar and we followed Ken as he searched out the white with green accents of the BASE-Duvel team car. Peter flagged us down only about two hundred meters after the start line. He had found himself in a nice spot in front of a house.

We handed him our bags and I began to pin on my number to my jersey. The weather had started to improve, with the rain only a light mist, but only slightly, as the temperature was still staying firmly chilly at fifty degrees. The sun was breaking through the clouds in a few spots, shooting rays of light intermittently in a sporadic spectacle of lights. I was ready for this, I knew it!

Peter began to address the group as we pinned on our numbers.

"Okay, guys, today is your first race here in Belgium. It's an old race, well established, and very hard. The weather isn't the best, but it's typical Belgium. The riders will go hard, so ride to the front of the race. It's no use being toward the back, especially in this weather. Go hard and do your best. Today is about learning the racing style and gaining some experience. You will have about four other teammates out there. See if you can find them before the race and introduce yourselves. I am almost sure they all speak English. Any questions?"

I looked around but no one was saying a word, and I wasn't planning on saying anything either.

I started off down the road but turned around after only five hundred meters. I didn't want to get too far away from the starting area, as I didn't want to miss the start of my race. The anticipation was killing me and I went back over to see what Peter was doing and ask him about feeding during the race.

When I reached Peter he was reading a piece of paper in his hand. I asked him, "What is that?"

"This? This is the start list. There are one hundred and sixteen riders today, a good showing."

"Oh, well, what do we do about feeding?"

"There will be an older gentleman, Dwergje, with a mustache in a team jersey about three kilometers down the road where there is a slight rise. If you need a feed yell at him. But with the weather this cold you shouldn't need one today. Now get back to the start line before the race goes off and leaves you."

I then noticed the bustle of activity around me, and the adrenaline started to pump: it was start time!

"Okay, thanks. See you after the race!"

I lined up at the start line about three rows back. There were so many racers and we were crammed in between the barriers like cattle. I stood there waiting as an official stood in front of us and made some announcements. I looked around at the riders around me. These guys weren't plump with a cushion of fat under their skin. Almost every rider was lean, skin pulled taut against their frames, exposing the definition of muscles and a network of coursing veins. I steadied my thoughts, tightened my grip on the handlebars, and let out a large breath of calm. I waited for the start of the race.

It all began with the lowering of a green flag. As the ripples of green fell, the riders were off in an instant. I accelerated my pedal stroke to overtake a couple of riders before the first right-hand bend. There were still a good thirty riders ahead of me, but I was satisfied with knowing there were more riders behind than ahead.

The riders began to single file out in instantaneous reaction to the speed. As quickly as the field elongated it was crunched back together quickly as we hit the first left-hand corner. The riders were braking cautiously then sprinting out the corners to catch the draft of the rider ahead of them. I had never ridden with riders who went so slow into clean corners. I held my own through the field, but the speed wasn't letting up.

Typically in the U.S., this was about the point where everyone had accelerated to his desired position and in unconscious collective agreement the pace settled down. Today, this was not the case, as my lactic-laden legs began to ache as the twinges of pain still lingered in the muscles. The field continued its painful pace as we turned left and right through the outskirts of Oudenaarde.

It was as we left the shelter of the buildings that I felt the true, torturous nature of the peloton. A right-hand bend led the peloton onto a small road, smaller than some golf cart paths I have ridden, that exposed the peloton to a large farm field. There were no trees, no buildings, nothing to inhibit the wind's full force from pushing me farther into pain. The wind was coming strongly from the right, with the peloton hugging the left edge of the road, leaving no room to hide from the wind. I pushed as hard as I could and made it onto the wheel in front of me, but I could feel little relief.

Finally, the field turned to the right and the strife was suspended. The front slowed up and the field was bunched up again. I was stuck in the middle of a mass of riders, nowhere to move. No amount of handling skills would get me an inch farther in this cluster of riders. I watched as three riders accelerated off the front and people sat there unmoved. I wanted to jump across the riders and attack after them, but even if I were in the position of the riders in front of me I couldn't have gone. I needed to recover from the crosswind and try to survive till we arrived back to the city; the race was only just beginning.

Another right-hand corner led the peloton onto a large main road, and I could see the three lead riders ahead of the field with a lead of maybe five hundred meters. The road was wide, but it didn't help at all. Immediately the riders at the front moved to the right and let the crosswind work its evil on the field. We were all pinned against the right-hand side of the road, trying to ride on the absolute edge in hopes of catching just a little relief from the wind.

During this whole time I hadn't even noticed any other riders. Hell, not even the scenery. I was in survival mode; all I wanted to do was make it to the end! I looked up from the wheel to notice the rider in front of me struggling. I couldn't believe it; only one lap into the race and there were guys falling off by the wayside. He started to fade another foot and I was worried. I didn't have the power to accelerate around him.

Right when I thought all hope was lost, I saw a hand extend backwards. No words were exchanged, but my history on the velodrome instinctively led me to reach out and grab the hand. The rider felt my grasp and in a solid swing threw me right onto the next wheel. I dared not look back and couldn't even yell out thanks to him. I just gritted my teeth and dug a little deeper into my reserves. The finish line lay in front of me, a relief to see, but I was only on lap one. There were ten more laps to go.

As we passed the finish line I saw Sergei come past me on my left. I didn't know how he was going, but I didn't care, as his huge frame would provide an excellent draft. In a quick and solid motion I moved into his draft and continued on. The second lap was a repeat of the first, the third a repeat of the second. It wasn't until lap four that I felt the true odious speed of the race.

After the third lap I was feeling better. Most of the lactic had worked its way out and the speed was slightly slower. The field had just caught the original breakaway of three riders just after the finish line. The field made its way out of the town with the speed very high in straights and slowing perpetually in the corners as the rain started to pick up. At the right-hand bend onto the open farm fields, death began. I was already in pain and feared this section. The turn came and I felt the resistance increase immensely against my legs.

The slow death of lactic acid grew from a small pain in my left leg and migrated its way outward. Similar pain began to brew in my right leg as the pace continued. I focused on the wheel in front of me and told myself I wasn't going to get dropped from my place. The pain continued, but I endured and kept on going. The pace slowed up a little just before the right-hand bend into the headwind, and I was grateful. After the bend I looked up for the first time since we entered the crosswind section. Only four riders were in front of me.

I looked up the road to see a group of around twenty riders ahead of everyone. I wasn't prepared to be dropped and accelerated from my position toward the front. I tried with all that was in my legs, but the lead group kept increasing its lead. I pulled off and signaled the riders behind me to chase, but they shot back blank stares. I couldn't pull the riders back alone.

I faded back to the rear of the group. There were riders struggling to re-establish contact with the peloton and I saw Troy just latch on as I arrived at the rear of the field. I looked over at him and I could see the pain in the cringes of his eyes. The look told me all I needed to know.

The rest of the race was an uninspiring attempt to reestablish contact with the front group. I would follow riders as they attacked only to have them stop mere minutes later, then another attack would follow and those riders would follow through. There was little to truly no logic in the way things were developing. I tried to follow what I thought would make it, but it didn't work.

Eventually the group was whittled down to a small group of about ten. Some riders were ahead on the course, others had packed it in long ago. As we approached the finish line with two laps to go, an official was standing on the side of the road with a red flag. I knew what was going on: we were done. I sprinted in vein for some unknown spot.

I gingerly rolled over to the car where Peter was, and, debilitated, I dismounted my bike. Troy was already there in warm, fresh clothes. Peter came over to me and put his hand on my back.

"Well, that wasn't bad. Pretty good for your first European race."

I looked up at him in bewilderment with my face covered in the grit and filth of the road.

"Good? That was terrible. I didn't even finish the race!"

"No, you didn't finish the race, but you were in there for almost all of it. Anyways, it's early; give yourself some time. Success isn't instantaneous. It's a long process of cumulative time focused on one goal where you improve your weaknesses and capitalize your strengths. Trust my judgment; your time will come."

I didn't care to hear such words. I was in total disbelief at how utterly hard the riders rode.

Peter interrupted my inner monologue of criticism, "Andy, don't forget to return your number after the race. You get money back, and if you don't do it you will be fined by the federation. Okay?"

"Okay, where do I turn it in?"

"The same place you registered; it's not always that way, but it is this time."

I nodded in acknowledgment and began to put on some dry clothing and a rain cape.

I watched Ken and Sergei race by as I was pulling a clean jersey over my head. Ken was in the lead group of eight riders and Sergei was in the group behind that break with seven riders. I was impressed to see them up there, because back home I was able to pull off some decent results and here I was not even finishing a local Belgian race!

In the end, a lone rider broke off the front of the breakaway and soloed in for the win. Ken was able to pull off a fifth place and Sergei was a solid twelfth. There were two other BASE-Duvel riders in the top twenty, but I didn't take much notice with my personal preoccupation with my pathetic performance.

The ride home was long, but it was good to flush out the massive amounts of byproduct buildup in my legs. We all arrived at the house just before dark and I silently went to my room. I thought a hot shower would make me feel better, but it didn't. I inhaled a large bowl of pasta and a whole chicken breast for dinner, more food than I had consumed in a long while. I felt drained. I felt tired. I didn't feel much like a cyclist.

I returned to my room to find Troy laying in bed and reading a book. I lay down on my bed and propped my legs up against the wall and started to work out the problem areas. I leaned my head a little farther back over the edge of the bed and looked at Troy on the other side of the room.

Peering at his upside-down image I asked, "What do you think of the race today?"

"It was hard. It was really hard."

"Did you expect that?"

"Not really. I thought I might be able to finish, but the crosswind was so strong."

Grabbing his thin thighs he said, "Plus, these legs aren't power factories. I'm never going to be a true flatlander."

"Well, I am a power rider and it killed me. I wasn't ready for that."

"I've had many people tell me about racing here, but hearing a story of the race's pain for ten hours could not compare to even ten seconds of the experienced pain."

"You're telling me."

With that I let Troy return to his reading. I felt this might be the end, but I knew there was more within me. The race had been a slap in my face, an epiphany into the reality of the brutality inherent to European racing. I wanted more; my true limits weren't reached. Physically I wasn't able to go harder, but mentally I wanted to continue, to go on. I needed to bide my time and wait for my physical ability to catch up.

I let my legs slide down the wall and land on the bed with a large thump. I lay on my back and looked to the ceiling and smiled. My mind drifted into a solemn sleep. My body needed some serious rest after the day's draining race.

* * *

I walked out of the shed and emerged from the alley to see a familiar face: Frank Williams. Frank and most of the Xerox team riders were in Europe for a three-week European campaign. Xerox Europe wanted to get some extra publicity and stir up some excitement, so they put up the money and flew the team to Europe.

"Frank! How ya doin'?"

"I'm fantastic. I'm in fine form and I am excited to ride some of the old roads of Belgium. How about you?"

"Oh things are okay … the racing is harder than I expected, but I like it, makes you hurt and suffer. I've done four Kermesse races in the last three weeks but I haven't finished one. I think I might have finished Wednesday's Kermesse, but I flatted an hour into the race."

"That's a total bummer. So what you want to do for a ride?"

"Oh, nothing special, just an easy coffee shop ride. I want to be fresh for tomorrow's race."

"Okay then, I know of a nice quiet coffee shop in Brakel I'd like to visit. De Nevel it's called."

"Sounds like a fine place … let's roll."

Frank and I strolled leisurely meandering our way though the streets of Gent. He talked about the winter and how everything was going in his life. I listened with eagerness about the winter training and the recent races he completed in Europe. The Xerox team was mainly racing in Northern France, Belgium, Holland, and Luxembourg. They had just finished a weekend of back to back UCI 1.2 races in France with Frank and teammate Daniel Parson taking third and seventh, respectively, on the first day. The second day was an exceptional day as Daniel, the team's best sprinter, took the field sprint and the win. The result translated instantly into respect for the team, but better yet, some well-deserved invitations to some big races, including a prestigious UCI 1.HC in Belgium this weekend.

I was in the middle of my inner monologue when Frank broke the silence.

"Pedaling along the back roads of Belgium is a welcome relief to the stress of the roads of the U.S. Out here you can truly get lost, both physically and in your mind. I remember doing rides out here for hours and seeing only a few cars pass."

Looking over to me he said, "So, Andy, what are your thoughts so far about Europe?"

"It strangely feels like home. I don't really feel out of place; in fact, I think I feel almost more in place here than the U.S. The other day I was talking with our butcher, Fritz, about the weekend's race and about things going on in cycling. After I left I thought about it: I had never once had a discussion like that with any non-cyclist in the U.S." I paused for a second then continued. "It's like people here understand me … and respect what I do. I never felt that in the U.S. with people I knew. Few people back home respect the sacrifices and challenges a cyclist faces. Here, they do."

I looked at Frank expecting a response, but none came; all I could get out of him was a fine, faint grin. I continued rambling on about the house and all the things that were so different in Belgium than in the U.S. The way toilet seats had flush levers that you had to pull up on and not a handle. The way TV shows just cut from one segment to another because they didn't add in as many commercials to the shows. Frank just laughed and added in his comments and anecdotes as we made our way to Brakel.

Once in Brakel, Frank led the way to De Nevel, hidden on a side street off the town's center. The café had a nice courtyard out front with a beautiful view of the town's church across the square. We leaned our bikes against the wrought-iron fence of the veranda and sat down for a nice coffee. The day was perfect and picturesque, with clear blue skies, chilly air but not cold temperatures and a bright sun casting crisp shadows over the old brick buildings of Brakel.

We each ordered some coffee, sat back, and relaxed. These were the moments I really enjoyed, second to the racing, of course—the times where I was able to just sit back and let time seem to slow to a crawl. The moments would hang frozen in my mind, where I could study and appreciate their beauty. I was in Europe, racing my bike, living a dream, and pursuing my life's passion. I was living my life fully.

From my personal daze I heard Frank talking, " … ready to go?"

"Huh?"

"Are you ready to go?"

"Yes, I am ready … ready for the journey."

* * *

"*Aalter*—the place of race." Sergei's deep, bellowing voice continued, "Leave you in a state of paranoia—Ooh, don't make a move for your gat so soon 'cuz I drops bombs like *Platoon*.—Snoop Dogg is da man! We gonna kill today."

I did all I could to keep from laughing myself to death. Sergei's knowledge of random rap quotes was a constant source of amusement in the house. He would always have his headphones on, walking around the house, spouting off line after line. Which, under normal circumstances, wouldn't be interesting, but seeing a six-foot-plus Russian doing it, well, that is priceless.

Everyone was gathered around the kitchen table for breakfast, bantering away about the day's race.

Ken started off, "Today we get to take one of the team cars. Alter isn't that far of a ride, but some local sponsors will be there, so Peter wants us to be fresh for the race."

Troy jubilantly put his hand on Sergei's shoulder, "Today I say we let the big man go to the front and shred the field to pieces. He's like a train out there steamrolling over the competition."

I added, "Yeah, but we have to suffer the same wrath, so I'm glad he's on our side."

Ken finished, "Well, today it would be nice to do well; just race smart and let's make some of the sponsors happy."

We arrived at the race early and with plenty of time to burn, so I walked over to the café for a coffee. Inside they hadn't even set up the registration for the race, but despite the small number of people, the smoky haze was still persistent, so I took my coffee to some small tables outside.

I sat down and sipped slowly on my coffee. The town's buildings were an assortment of Birkenstock browns, dark crimsons, and battleship grays that typified most all of Belgium. The race start was near the town square with a short patch of cobblestones, but they weren't the large "kinder koppen" of the famous races. These were smaller ones, tightly fitted neatly together in a fan-shaped pattern. Ken said they were called "klinker koppen" because they made your chain clink when you rode over them. I wasn't worried about their sounds but rather the effect water would have on their traction, though it wouldn't be a factor with the clear skies for today's race.

In fact, the nice weather had been lingering for the last two weeks. Only one rainy day, and the temperatures were cool but completely bearable. The trees were showing their first signs of budding, adding a nice green tone to the earthy array of the landscape and filling the surroundings with new life.

I too was feeling anew. With each race I was beginning to understand and develop a feel for the racing style. My first race in Belgium was a jagged pill that was so large I almost choked on it. But I endured, swallowed hard, and stomached the defeat with much discomfort. The second and third races were better. Only a minor discomfort in swallowing those pills. Then there is my last race; I actually enjoyed taking that pill. Its nature had turned from a discomfort to a pleasurable sense. I can only attribute this to Frank's theory of cyclists being sadistic. I was learning to love pain and accept something my bodily fibers told me to be dire. I emerged from my chair and returned to the team vehicle to start to get dressed.

The commencement of seventy-six racers to 115 kilometers of pain began promptly at three o'clock in the afternoon. The field accelerated in haste toward the first corner as people collided for their place in the peloton. As we approached the first right-hand bend, I was ready for the flow of the riders and counteracted the leisurely entry into the corner of the other riders by cutting to the inside. I generated quite a few *godverdommes*, the all-encompassing Flemish curse word, with my maneuvers, but the efforts landed me at the front and I was saving oodles of energy from the constant accelerations.

I found the farther I rode to the front the less the yo-yo effect had on me. I would notice riders at the front go purposely slow through corners to cause the effect, making life hell on the riders at the back. The other great enlightenment I had at the last race was finding the right wheels. Coming to Belgium I didn't know Jurgen from Jan, so I waited around the start finish area to see the odds the bookies gave. I didn't have time to learn everyone who was anyone with over five hundred riders in Belgium and then see if they were at the race. So I let the bookies do the job for me. I figured anyone who had single digits for the win multiplier was a good wheel, and riders with anything below three were going to be a "sure bet." Today's race I marked three riders, numbers thirteen, twenty-seven, and thirty-four. Each had less than five for their win multiplier. My odds were thirty to one for the win and fifteen for the top three. Not great.

The field made its way through the outskirts of the city as we dodged traffic pylons that lined the side of the road in various sections. The first lap went by without much of anything important happening, but on the second lap things started to heat up. I watched the marked riders and noticed number twenty-seven starting to make his way up the right side of the field. I took note and made my way in his direction.

Right as I rolled up behind his wheel he attacked. I was prepared for the acceleration and quickly caught onto his wheel. The speed was bearable but extremely fast. He took his pull and I followed through with a hard pull of my own. As I faded back I assessed the situation: there were six of us off the front, one other BASE-Duvel teammate, but I didn't know him, and the peloton was chasing hard behind us. I had made my first bona fide breakaway in Europe. I hoped that my teammates would take advantage of the situation by saving energy while helping toward the breakaway's success.

As I pulled forward in the rotation, I yelled to my unknown teammate, "Hey there, you ready for this?"

He nodded and hollered, "Do your fair share of the work, American!"

I was taken aback by the statement. I didn't know him and he didn't know me. So who was he to assume such things? I ignored his comment and kept moving along in the rotation. As I took my second pull, I could feel the burn starting in my legs. I took a couple of deep breaths and relaxed to lower my heart rate. There was a long way to go in the race.

After the second lap was completed I knew there were some primes for money each lap, and with the sponsors present I wanted to show off a bit and also for my unknown teammate. The breakaway continued its drive, and the flow was smooth for the most part, everyone taking his fair share of the work.

The approach to the finish was straight and long but had a sharp right-hand bend only a couple hundred meters after the finish. The wind was only a whisper from the right, so either side was a viable option for making an attack for the finish. Everyone looked to be fresh and I didn't know what to expect as we approached.

To my surprise the speed on the finishing straight was hard, but not very high. With three hundred meters to go I jumped from my fourth spot in line and easily took the sprint. I slowed down to wait for the rest of the field and heard some commotion from behind.

"Godverdomme, dwaze Amerikaan!"

I glared back at the rider, but held my tongue. I knew not the words, but the tone told me all I needed. As I retook my place in the break my unknown teammate come up next to me.

"Hey! You don't do that. We share the work and the money. No mess up the turns, okay?"

"So you don't sprint here?"

"Not when everyone works; need to keep up the speed."

"Okay, won't happen again."

I felt a bit embarrassed by my faux pas, but that was part of the learning process. I persisted, trucking right along, and as I passed the rider who had just yelled at me I gave assurance to him that it wouldn't happen again. Glaring back at me he said nothing. The breakaway was moving right along and we were maintaining our lead, but we were never fully out of sight of the peloton. They maintained a close proximity that left me uncomfortable about the breakaway's success.

The breakaway continued its collusion all the way to the bitter end, but after a little over an hour and half off the front we were reeled in by the peloton. I played my hand of cards and it didn't pan out. The field reshuffled the deck and within the same lap a new group had split off the front. I wasn't in a state to chase, so I buried myself in the field and let myself recuperate from my effort.

I looked around to see who was still left in the field. Ken and Troy both had missed out on the breakaway. Ken came over to me to talk.

"Andy, good job with the break. Just hang in and finish the race out. We can rest, as Sergei and another BASE-Duvel rider are up the road."

"Sweet! I need to rest; that was some hard riding."

"Okay, just keep out of the wind."

The rest of the race went by quickly in a blur of memory. I let my mind relax and the time flew by, and before I knew it, I heard the announcer yelling, *"Laatste Ronde, Laatste Ronde."* It was a beautiful sound, the words for the last lap of the race. I wasn't going to be dropped, no matter the pain induced into my legs.

I kept my place in the field, around midway in the peloton, but by this point the field was whittled down to about thirty or so riders, with fewer than ten guys off the front. I didn't want to risk going with any breakaways and getting dropped, so I put my money on whatever my legs could produce in the field sprint.

The lead-up to the finish was long and the attacks came well before four kilometers to go. Guys seemed intent on going the long way to the finish and didn't want to deal with the chaos of a mass finish.

Two guys were able to make their way off the front, but the peloton maintained its mass form all the way to the finish.

The long straightaway gave the riders at the front the opportunity to drill the pace into the mid-thirty-mile-an-hour range for the entire length of the approach, which they fully employed. I wasn't able to muster much of a deadly sprint, but had enough to finish around fifth in the field sprint. Ken was right behind me, and I believe Troy made it in with the field. I rolled to a stop and apathetically made my way over to the finish area. I was tired, I was torn up inside, but I had a smile spanning the entire length of my salt-encrusted face. I had finished my first European race!

At the start-finish area, I saw the winner of the race. It was number thirteen, one of the marked riders. The bookies sure knew how to pick them.

Peter greeted me with a big smile, "Your first finish and you won two primes! It's been a good day for you, Andy."

I kept grinning. Peter handed me a wet washrag and a bottle of cold water to wash myself and introduced me to some of the sponsors. They seemed pleased with the day's results. Sergei was third in the end, another teammate was sixth, and I placed in the top twenty. In all, it was a great race for the team and myself.

Peter addressed the riders, "Guys, today you all did a wonderful job. Things are going very well for the team and we are giving the larger teams a hard time. Let's keep this up. I also have some more good news. Tomorrow is the Ronde Van Vlaanderen. Mr. De Smet here has arranged to get any rider who wants it a pass inside the rider's area. You can go and see the riders up close and personal."

As if racing wasn't exciting enough, to be able to enter the rider area of the most famous of all Belgian races, that was amazing. Jurgen's countless tales of the Tour of Flanders alluded to the great reverence this race entailed, and I was going to be able to see and experience that reverence up close and personal.

After Peter's little speech, a Belgian teammate came up to me. He was the rider I was with in the breakaway.

"American, you did good today. You have some things to learn, but it was good riding. My name is Frans De Wouwer. I will see you around the races."

"Thanks, I'm Andy Bennet. I'll be around."

It was nice to have some respect from my Belgian teammates. The four of us from the apartment were outsiders to all the other riders, foreigners here to take spots away from them and their friends.

I collected my prize money: fifteen euros for seventeenth place in the race and twenty euros for the primes. It wasn't the most money I had made at a bike race by far, but it was certainly the hardest-earned money I had ever made. The money I held in my hand was more valuable than the worth printed on the bills; it was tangible validation of my developing fitness and my ability to improve and succeed.

V—Progression & Regression

I had been to Brugge before. It was a favorite ride of mine to take the canal over to the Venice of the North for a nice cup of coffee and enjoy the five-hundred-year-old buildings. But today was different; today I was to experience the most famous of all the Belgian races. The only other single-day race to hold more allure was Paris-Roubaix, but I wouldn't have told any of these fans that today. This day was theirs, the people's race, and a national obsession.

Cycling in Belgium is the people's sport. Unlike the other national sport, soccer, cycling was free and accessible to everyone, which gives cycling its media and fanfare appeal. We took the team car to Brugge, parked at the train station, and walked the rest of the distance to the start of the race at the market square. People were migrating en mass, as if attracted by a huge magnet. As I turned the corner around the large, red cultural arts building, I saw an abundance of team buses. There were tons of them, all lining the fenced-off area in the market square. I was at a real live World Cup race. During my summer of racing with Track Stand Racing nothing ever came close to this, and the only event in America I could think of that could come close was the USPRO champs in Philadelphia, but even that was a minor blip compared to this spectacle.

Ken got on his GSM and called up the sponsor from the day before to come and meet us by the entrance where the Rabobank team was located. After he got off the phone, I started to hear a large chorus of voices. It kept going on and on, and I listened harder. It was coming from the fence area near the Cofidis bus next to the Rabobank bus. I walked over to see a large group of white T-shirt-clad guys all chanting away.

In a male-testosterone mob they ranted, "NICO MATTAN, NICO MATTAN, NICO MATTAN ..."

It was craziness; they were grown men all cheering for a bicycle racer.

As I got closer I noticed the back of the T-shirts read "Nico Mattan Ultras—Supporters Club." It was the coolest thing I had seen all year. A rider with his own personal fan club! There were even guys carrying a large banner bearing Nico's last name, and everyone kept chanting till finally, after a couple of minutes, Nico emerged from the team bus. He said a few lines to them, momentarily calming down the frenzy, and then went inside.

I couldn't believe the way people were. I was seeing people wearing team jerseys, little kids with "De Leeuw Van Vlaanderen" Johan Museeuw shirts, and average people showing up in droves for the start of a bike race. I walked back over to the entrance to the rider area just as the sponsor arrived with our inside passes. He led us inside and introduced us to the Relax-Bodysol riders. He was also a sponsor of that team and that was the reason we could get inside today.

The riders were really nice, but I didn't ask much more than what their names were, as I didn't want to disturb them. I started to wander off and look around at all the riders' busses and bikes. Some of the teams, mostly the Division II squads, had nothing more than glorified camper trucks as their team busses, and on the other end of the spectrum you had top-level Division I teams with huge, elaborate busses. I was surprised to see such a disparity in the busses, but I guess the bus mattered not; it was the rider's legs that mattered.

I was walking around seeing riders in the flesh I had only seen in magazines or on TV. There were Tour de France stage-winners, guys who were ex-world champions, riders that had won the RVV before, and even some great riders of the past who had assumed managerial roles among the teams. I had met professional riders in the U.S. before and had even raced against almost every single domestic professional, but this was different. These guys were the top European professionals; it was like playing triple-A baseball and then moving up and meeting the guys you had trading cards of growing up. Only difference was I wasn't moving up to the majors; I was a minor leaguer at a big game.

I continued to walk around and view the spectacle, as a rider's jersey flashed in front of my very eyes, silver and light blue with world championship stripes on the sleeve. I took more notice and I could see it was Johan Museeuw, the Lion of Flanders himself. As he passed, the people would start an incredible cheer, and the uproar followed him as he went up and down the road between the starting area and myself. It was crazy how the people reacted; it was like he was rock star, a cycling rock star!

I saw the voice of cycling himself, Phil Ligget, and his associate Paul Sherwen. They were doing pre-race interviews. I mean it was the man himself, Phil. I looked around as if this were a dream. My dreams were filled with these real events. People cheering on riders, amassed to pay homage to the great two-wheeled warriors of the roads. I knew this was something I wanted. I desired and longed to be part of this dream.

Troy came over to me.

"Man, this is something else. You will never guess who I just met."

"I don't know, everyone who is anyone in cycling?"

"Yeah, it's so cool!"

Troy then scurried off to go and see more riders before they left for the start. I looked at my watch and it was fifteen till the ten o'clock start.

I looked around and found Ken still talking to some of the Relax-Bodysol riders. He was in conversation with a rider who was double-checking his bike before the start while talking at the same time. The fluidity with which he did both was a testament to his professionalism. It came as naturally to him as breathing and blinking. The rider finished a quick brake adjustment and he was off. Ken came over to me.

"You ready to get going? Everyone will be gone in three minutes, and this way we can get home in time to ride to the *Muur.*"

"Wait, you mean The Muur, the famous one from this very race?"

"Yup, we can ride down there and sit in one of the café's till the race gets close, then rush outside to see the race go up the climb. It's complete chaos, but it's worth the trip."

"Really? That would be awesome."

We rounded up the rest of the guys and all made our way back to Gent. The race still had four hours till it would be at *De Muur* in Geraardsbergen, so we relaxed and ate a little lunch before our ride. As we left the apartment, there was a small break of three guys who had a sizeable fifteen-minute lead over the peloton. They were all from smaller teams, looking to ensure some TV time for their sponsors, with a slim chance of holding their lead to the end for a victory.

The whole way down, we all debated and placed our own little bets on who would win. My personal selection was Van Petegem, who had already won two races this year. Ken selected Johan Museeuw based solely on this being his last year as a racer in the peloton. Troy chose Eric Dekker from Rabobank, while Sergei went nationalistic with fellow Russian Viatcheslav Ekimov. We all agreed that if anyone was right the other guys had to clean their bike once as payment. The talk and debate passed the time quickly to De Muur.

We arrived over an hour and half before the race was scheduled to pass through, which was good 'cause in less than an hour the entire area would be overrun with cycling-mad fans. Once there we found a little café to hide out in from the cold, grab a warm drink while watching the race on TV. The race was developing as a small, select group was being methodically formed through consistent discretion of the many cobbled, and uncobbled, burgs of the race palmarès.

As it stood, it looked like Troy and Ken were going to have a chance of winning the bet, but there was still an hour left in the race, and there were still a few more hard hills to face. I couldn't get over how out of the ten or so different Belgian bars I had been in, they all seemed to be made out of the same mold, all complete with late-seventies-cliché decor. This bar was stuck in the same time warp as the rest of Belgium.

The jubilant owner of the bar noticed us sitting at the table dressed in our cycling clothing and started to talk to us. He was very impressed that we had all come such a long way to race in Belgium and even more so that we were here in his bar to watch the grand Ronde Van Vlaanderen. He went on about the greats of cycling and about watching Eddy Merckx win a Kermesse in Oudenaarde back when he was a very young man, and the times he passed this very bar on his way to win the same race on TV, but back when he was just a teenager and his father owned the bar.

The race was nearing and we all got up to leave.

As we asked for the bill the owner looked at us and said, "No, today it's my treat. You paid me with stories of your travels here. Enjoy the race."

Everyone but Ken couldn't believe this reaction. We all thanked him immensely and left for the infamous De Muur. The climb was extremely steep and we had to fight our way through the masses of people to find a decent spot. Trying to climb onto the side of the road's incline in cleats was a challenge, but we managed well enough.

Within fifteen minutes people were packed in wall to wall while drinking, eating, and having a merry old time. Some had on radios and the more prepared even had TVs and picnics set up for watching the race. All these people waiting for just a glimpse of riders as they passed; a brief twenty-second rendezvous of an over-six-hour race. This, however, was the spot where so many riders had translated themselves from a placer into a winner. The weaning of the weak provided a splendid spectacle where you were able to see full the exquisite pain and grimace of every facial crevice gleaming with beads of sweat, as audible cringes of malice erupted from deep within the throes of the body's agony.

The entire climb was lined with barricades with people pressed squarely against them, and in places ten people deep. The crowd started into a frenzy as the first of the course marshal vehicles passed. The riders were within minutes of De Muur and the anticipation in the crowd was radiating into the air. There were people chanting away with Belgian drinking songs, crazy guys waving the eminent yellow and black flag of Flanders, and the general chaos of any sports crowd.

The first group to come by was a small, six-rider field of upper-echelon classics riders. It was amazing to watch them tackle the acclivitous incline in powerful pedal stokes. Each of them dominated the cobbled domain, but it was Dekker who mastered it. He pedaled in simplistic smoothness. I watched him pass mere feet in front of my eyes with *the* look on his face, unyielding determination. He was deep within the grip of pain, but he was the one in control, the one controlling the pain.

He distanced himself over the apex of the berg and never looked back. Dekker soloed his way all the way to the finish in spectacular fashion as the rest of the breakaway looked at each other for the first antagonistic movement, which came too late to be of any use. We watched all of it from small battery-powered, thirteen-inch TVs crowded by at least forty people on the side of the Muur.

On the way back, Troy went into explicit detail about all the special ways we needed to clean his bike and was milking his race prediction for all it was worth. We rode back to the apartment before darkness encompassed the streets, and relaxed the rest of the night after our long day of adventure.

* * *

I was sitting on the floor in the living room early Wednesday morning doing a little stretching when there was a knock at the door. I opened it to find Peter Ververken softly smiling at me with his slim lips. I invited him inside and asked if he wanted something to drink but he declined.

He then asked, "So is Ken home?"

I said, "No, Ken is out on a ride, but I believe Troy and Sergei are still home."

"Oh, okay … well, I'll just tell you and you can relay the message to the rest of the guys. I am in a hurry to do some team business. This weekend you guys will be racing in Hasselt in the Wallonia region of Belgium. It is a UCI 1.6–ranked race, so there will be some very fast teams there, and the region is hilly with some of the same hills as *La Flèche Wallonne.*"

"Wow! Really? We get to do a UCI race?"

"Yup, the racing is picking up and you guys are doing well, so you all are selected for this weekend's race."

"Great, I'll tell the guys!"

"Okay, take care … I'm off."

I was speechless at the prospect of my first UCI race. These were the top-level races and were supposed to be harder and longer than Kermesses. The excitement outweighed the hints of doubt that lingered in my head. This was my chance to bring my abilities to a new level, where the prospect of placement in the pro peloton was possible. I bolted over to tell Troy and Sergei the good news.

Ken seemed indifferent to the news. He took it in his usual good-natured calm, accustomed to his disposition. He nodded solemnly in acceptance and continued silently on to his room. The guys in the house had all up to this point been doing only Kermesse races, so I thought Ken would have been excited like Troy and Sergei.

The days leading up to the race, I was growing ever nervous about the race. I remembered some of the climbs from the videos I had seen over the years, but what would it be like racing over them? I filled the kilometers of my rides with simulated scenarios in my head to ease my mind. The role-playing let my mind work out the reaction I would have if a circumstance would happen for real. I knew the situations that would arise in the U.S., but here in Europe I was learning a completely different style of racing that was as extraneous to me as the language of Flemish.

The morning of the race, I was packing my bag into the team car when Troy came over to me.

"You ready for this?"

I was in a delightful mood and without hesitation I boldly stated, "Ready? Hell, I was born ready!"

"Yeah, that's what I am talking about!"

Troy saw Sergei coming down the stairs from the apartment.

"Sergei, what we gonna do to the other racers today?"

"You see I'm quick to let the hammer go click on my Tec-9 … so if you try to wreck mine, fool it's your bad time!"

Troy and I laughed so hard at the Russian Express's linguistic knowledge of rap. Not to be outdone, I pulled out a great line out of my extensive memory bank of movie quotes.

"You're best? Losers always whine about their best. Winners go home and fuck the prom queen."

Ken came out of the apartment and put his bag in the car without saying a word. In fact, he drove the whole way to the race saying only what was needed to ask for help with the directions left by Peter. The rest of us kept talking about the past week's racing, people we thought would be at the race, and who was doing well. We were learning each other's strengths and weaknesses and forming the needed knowledge for unspoken communication essential for cohesion within a team.

Hasselt is a beautiful town deep in the Wallonia region of Belgium. I gazed through the window at the undulating scenery, and for a brief moment I had a flashback and I thought I was back in Boone on my way to a race. It was the first time in five weeks that I had thought of home. The thought made me miss some of the comforts of home, but it was only a thought, as I wanted to be exactly where I was at that very moment. I took it as a sign that my life was going in the right direction; my present path is my only focus and desire.

The race was slated to be a 150-kilometer race with two large and separate loops of forty-five kilometers and fifty-five kilometers and then five, ten-kilometer loops of a finishing circuit in the town. Peter explained the major obstacles would be three significant hills of over three kilometers in length coming at twenty-five, thirty-four, and seventy-eight kilometers into the race. The finishing circuit had one small hill in it, but it wasn't steep, just gradual. Peter went over the rest of the logistics of the race including protocol for calling up the car from the caravan, signing in before the race, what to do for a flat, and where the feed zones were located.

Peter finished the team meeting and let us begin our preparations for the race. I was sitting on the curb pinning on my number when a man came over with a camera. I looked up at the man; he was youthful, but not young and had the lines of experience marking his face.

He then looked at a piece of paper and asked, "Bennet, Andy?"

I glanced a whimsical look, "Umm ... Yes."

"Hi, can I make your picture?"

"Uh, sure that is fine."

I threw my jersey over my shoulders and zipped it up all the way. Rising up, my view of the man was better. Strands of his dark black hair fluttered sporadically over his plush face, which was accented with a dark mustache.

I stood upright and he had me adjust my jersey and stand just so before he snapped off a photo.

"Can you sign here please?"

I saw a list of riders and lots of signatures on the page, so I obliged. He smiled, causing his mustache lift upward at the sides.

"I am Jean-Paul Vanderhaegen. I am pleased to meet you. Do you really come from America?"

"Yes, I grew up in Pennsylvania, but have been living in Boone, North Carolina."

"And you come all this way to race bicycles?"

"Yup, I am in the country of cycling! This place is wonderful. I love how hard the racing is here. It makes me strong."

"In Belgium we have many great bike racers; it's very hard racing here."

He stopped for a second and then continued, "Mr. Andy Bennet, do you have a team Web site?"

"Not that I know of, but I can give you my e-mail. Would that work?"

"Yes ... that would be fine." I wrote down the address and he thanked me. "I must see other riders before the race start; thank you for the photo and signature."

He walked off and I looked over to Ken, who was grinning. He jousted a coy bit of verbiage.

"Looks like someone has a new friend ... don't worry, you just met the first of many Belgian Super-fans."

"Super-fans?"

"Yup, Belgian Super-fans ... at least that is what I call them. See, you got these old guys who seem to do nothing but go from race to race seeking out photos and signatures of all the racers. It's like a hobby of theirs, like collecting baseball cards for you Yanks."

"Well, it was a little weird."

"It's a cycling culture. People get the same way with football in England. Here it's cycling."

"I see ... cool! I have my first Belgian Super-fan!"

I continued with my usual pre-race preparations as I watched the team's soigneur Danny start to dispense quick pre-race massages to the guys. His name was Danny, but everyone on the team knew him as Dwergje. *Dwergje* was Flemish for a dwarf, but Danny was not that small, just overtly short. I liked Dwergje because he always was smiling and was so jubilant. I don't think I ever once saw the corners of his mouth drop below parallel.

Dwergje was always at the races. I had seen him around at almost every Kermesse save one, and he would feed the riders and always ask us if there was anything we needed. He always wore a team cycling cap with the bill turned up over his brown hair that always randomly protruded from under the cap. He had a large, rounded nose to match the plump, rounded face and rosy cheeks. He would start to sweat profusely during pre-race massages, as he put a lot of effort into his work.

After my massage, I finished getting ready and did a double-check on my bike one last time before the start. I didn't want anything to screw up my first UCI race.

As I was starting off for my warm-up, Sergei yelled out to me, "Andy, have you made signing?"

I couldn't understand what he meant and turned around to ask him face to face.

"Andy, have you made signing?"

"Huh?" "Sign in before race"

"Oh yeah, I gotta sign in at the start, right?"

"Yes."

"Thanks!"

In my haste to get ready, I had almost forgotten an essential part of the race: signing in. I was more nervous about the race start than I had thought, but I didn't let myself waste energy with internal debates of events that hadn't even happened. I soothed myself in the knowledge that this was what I had prepared for, I had come prepared, and I was ready for the challenge that lay before me.

On the start line I looked around to see teams from other countries and even national teams. The quality of the riders was definitely elevated over my previous races and our team wasn't one of the strongest ones here. Peter wanted us to sit back, conserve energy, and let the other teams do the brunt of the work in the race. It wasn't our place to go out and prove anything by killing ourselves at the front. There were plenty of larger teams for such brutal actions.

The start of the race went off in moderate tranquility. Everyone knew the distance and hills ahead, and we were intent on keeping things easy to start off. The first climb would be a critical point of the race and would tell me how my legs were going to compare to the rest of the field. I sheltered myself in the belly of the peloton and waited to see the nature of the beast's fury.

The tepid speeds gave way to caution in my gut and I felt a collective lust for increased velocity emanating from the riders. The first fifteen kilometers were at tempo, nothing to incite hurt into the legs, but quickly the gauntlet was thrown down and the race became alive. It started with the movement of three German National Team members up the right-hand side. They were attacking expediently on the sidewalk, dodging cars and curbs to gain advantage over the bloated peloton that engulfed the road. In precise fashion they weaved around various obstacles and pylons and advantaged themselves to the head of the race.

Once at the front the Germans proceeded to turn up the speed a couple of notches and strung the peloton out, slimming the peloton as everyone fought for fractions of relief from the increasing resistance. I watched the move happen and found a large rider to draft as we all hugged the right side of the road.

Preeminent hints of lactic acid started to seep into my legs as the speed was turned up another notch and the riders at the front rotated through. The pace continued for another two kilometers until a right-hand corner brought the field to a blunt point as the road narrowed and the riders filled in the little width the road provided. All the riders who wanted a top position were in place and well positioned for the climb to come. I was just breaking the top half of the peloton, and I tried my hardest to find a path to the front but there was none available. I was going to have to be content with my position and hope for the best on the climb.

I looked up the road and there were about eighty riders in front of me. This was such a large race, undertaking very small roads, so I knew I needed to gain some ground on the climb and make sure I was in better position so I would be ready for the fights to come. The approach to the climb saw riders using every available means to place themselves farther up in the group. One rider even tried to take a cyclocross route along the side of the peloton, but ended up catching his front wheel in a soft patch of dirt and slid down the side into a ditch. I held my ground and waited.

I watched as the first lead cars started the ascent to the top of the climb, but they disappeared behind the thick foliage of the trees, leaving the climb's total length obscured from view. As the peloton started to climb, I felt the speed slowing gradually, and by the time I actually started the climb the riders in front of me were going at a crawl's pace. I couldn't imagine how horrible the slowing speeds and even stoppage would hinder the riders behind me.

I instinctively shifted into my twenty-three-tooth cog and started to spin up the climb, steadily building my speed up and accelerating past a few riders at a time. I didn't know how long the rise would be. Peter said in the three- to four-kilometer range, but you just never know unless you knew the roads. The riders around me felt the grip of pain tighten, standing up to relieve the strained muscles and exhaling large, bellowing breaths as their bodies begged for more oxygen to move the mounting mounds of chemical byproducts infesting their legs. I could feel the twinge in my legs begin, but I ignored my body's calling for relief and continued my ascent.

One of the biggest advantages I possessed over the other riders in the peloton was my ability to spin, learned from my younger years of track racing. The track allowed only one gear, so anytime I wanted to accelerate or attack I had to do so through increased cadence. Spinning in the 120-rpm range for lengths of time was just a normal day's duty for a trackie.

The climb's slow, snakelike slope of the mountainside began to level off in gradient, and the front riders let themselves take a moment of relief from the pain. I used the pause and proceeded to click the rear derailleur down two gears and stood up for the first time since the beginning of the climb. I accelerated toward the front and planted myself into the top-twenty echelon of riders. I felt the terrible throbbing of the artery in my neck beat at an increasingly expedient rhythm as my effort came to a close. I had skirted my personal threshold of physical limits, but it was worth the effort for the prime position at the head of the peloton.

The descent was fast and sketchy as I careened down the unknown road before me cast in shadow. There were three teams, all unknown to me, at the front making life miserable for the rest of us. They were hell-bent on turning up the heat and melting away the fat padding the peloton, leaving only the lean meat to give a clear shape to the players of the peloton.

I pulled my weight firmly over the center of the bike, brought my chin close to my stem and focused my senses on the ever-changing conditions of the descent. The cold wind blew through my jersey, sending a chill over my body as it cooled the moisture built up from the just-completed effort. I followed the wheel in front of me as the group made its way onto road at the bottom of the descent. The riders began to pull through and I did my part and followed through, but dared not expend a watt of extra energy than I needed to complete the transition. There was a long way to go in the race, and I was in it for the long haul.

On the way back I found myself at the rear of our group after only fading back about twenty riders. I dared a glance back to see what carnage lay behind me only to find the rest of the field a full five hundred meters behind us, strung out, slightly organized, but still very much in an angry mood. The beast was still ready to strike. I looked around in the breakaway to assess the situation to find one Belgian BASE-Duvel rider and Troy had made it over the climb in the lead group. As I passed Troy on his return back and my way to the front, I gave him a quick thumbs-up to let him know I was there. On the way back he returned the signal.

We were barreling down the smooth, flat road with a river to our left. I was looking down at my cycle computer and I could tell the next climb was supposed to be coming up right now, but I looked up the distance to see only more flat road. Suddenly the race's lead vehicle took a quick turn to the right up a slope of road. I hadn't even seen the road it was so small. The climb began and the second dosage of lactic acid was dispensing its way through the legs of the peloton.

I felt my heart rate rise sharply in parallel with the gradient and I knew trouble was on the way. The high pace left little time for clearing the legs of waste and I was swimming in a cesspool of pain. I sat back on the saddle and gritted my teeth through the pain. After only one kilometer, I had to stand up, relieve the principal muscles, and shift the responsibility over to auxiliary muscles. I went through a new level of inner torment with each passing meter and, in spite of the pain, held my ground well. I followed the riders all the way to the bitter end and even crested the hill within a whisper of contact of the rear of the lead group, but I was shattered. The climb's fury pulled me to the brink of disaster and I acceded to the pain in my legs.

I tried in vain to hold the wheels of the few riders who made it over the top of the climb in front of the main peloton, but it would not happen. The peloton quickly overtook me and I faded into its girth of protection. I grabbed an energy bar out of the back of my jersey and tried to keep my body refueled and ready for more.

I had a mouthful of energy bar when Ken rolled up to me, "Mate, you were up there, what happened?"

I looked over at him and held up my half-eaten energy bar while pointing at my mouth. I waited till I was able to catch my breath to reply, "The hills … speed … killed me.…"

"Tough luck; who we got up there?"

Still recovering but not so out of breath I replied, "Troy and a Belgian … Troy is looking good … he might make it."

The rest of the race was a blur. The peloton chased, but they never regained contact with the lead of the race. I struggled over the top of the last climb, but hung on to the rear of the bunch. The rest of the race wasn't too bad. I did go back to the team car once in the race to get some bottles for the team to gain the experience of working my way around a race caravan.

The field kept pace and I would see a motorbike every so often with time checks, always in the four- to five-minute range, but never more. The lead held all the way to the finish. The sprint for the finish came, but I didn't even bother. I was utterly fatigued, and my legs wanted to rest. I finished my first UCI race, but it made me dig down deep inside, farther than ever before.

I rolled over to the team vehicles and sat down on the curb. I removed my helmet and drowned my head with the remnants of a cool bottle. I laid all the way back on the sidewalk and stared up at the bright blue skies. My body felt sore in places I never knew existed. As I looked up, I saw a man overhead as he obstructed most of my view. He leaned down. *"Alstublieft."* I stared up to see the team's soigneur, Dwergje holding out a wet towel to me.

I smiled up to him and accepted the moist, cool towel. It felt great against my salt- and grit-encrusted skin. Dwergje looked concerned.

"You be oke?"

I lay down on my back.

"Yes, I am fine, just totally guttered. I need a couple of minutes to just rest."

"Oke, Andy, good job to finish, de race was very hard."

I lay there as the rest of the team started to return from their post-race cool-downs. I didn't move for almost five minutes.

Once I got up I saw Troy standing in front of me with a very large smile on his face.

I impishly said, "You look like you just got laid."

"Didn't get laid, but feels nearly as good. I placed twelfth in the race today!"

Had I not been so tired I would have jumped to my feet at such news.

"Wow, that is awesome. You're a frickin' mountain goat."

"Yeah, well, chicken legs are good for some things."

"Yup, well good for ya."

I gradually arose, grabbed my bag, pulled out some food I had packed, and headed off for the showers.

The ride home was very short for me because as soon as we started off for home I was quickly soothed into sleep by the gentle rhythm of the road. Back at the apartment, I helped unpack the car and headed inside to lie down on the couch. I dropped into the ragged cushions with a large thud and a heavy sigh. I looked over at Ken sitting next to me. He drew a slight smile.

"Tough day, eh?"

"Yeah, I am ready to sleep for a week!"

"Welcome to the upper echelon of racing, Andy. The next step after races like that is the pro level. It's an important fact overlooked by most."

"Yeah, I know ... uh, Ken ...?"

I began to ask the question, but I didn't want to press the matter, so I stopped. Ken kept on.

"What is it, Andy?"

"Well ... today you were rather quiet the whole day. That's not really you; what was up?"

"Oh, well, I didn't want to tell you guys and have you worry. I had a nasty crash at the GP de Hasselt on a descent last year. The wreck put me off the bike for a week and really shook me up. There was no sense telling any of you about it going into your first UCI; there was enough for everyone to worry about."

The switch in my head clicked into the on position as to why Peter had asked for Ken first when he came over to tell us about the race.

Ken got up and returned to his room as I still lay on the couch not wanting to move a muscle. I spent five minutes just working up the energy to start thinking about getting up, then another five getting started. I made it to my bed and fell asleep the instant my head impacted the pillow. I slept a solid ten hours that night.

Two days later I received an e-mail from Jurgen.

Andy,

Glad to hear from a little birdie things are going well over in Belgium. I'm going to cut to the chase, as you know I don't mince my words. .

The big deal is not to lie to yourself. You have a job to do and you know how to do it. Again this is a tough job. It's a lot easier to look cool and not do the work. You have to push yourself to the max. Eat right, sleep right, have some fun, and train, train, train. Record your progress and study your diary. Think about what you're doing all the time. Please don't waste your time or bullshit around. This is a one-shot deal.

See how some of the older, stronger guys are working out. Guys that you know are tough. Ride with them and pick their brains. Stay away from any kind of pick-me-up. Some of these guys might be using stuff during their hard-training miles. That isn't a path you need ever take. The mind contains more training aid than any drug can provide.

I have faith in you, and believe me, I know all the pain involved. Either you do it or screw it. Results will only come when you really want them to. This is your new job. You can sweep the floor or be the boss. Be a pro on and off the bike. Make friends in the peloton. Most of all don't be an asshole. Cycling is a small world and bad news travels fast.

Last but not least, do it for Andy. That's what it's all about.

Your Friend,
Jurgen Van Roy

The words left me profoundly affected and invigorated with a renewed spirit after the energy drain I received in Hasselt. I was the master of my own destiny and I was going to get no more out of my life than that which I put into it.

* * *

I stared out the window to see two *gendarmerie* holding sub-machine guns. I tended to forget exactly how close in proximity things were in Europe and the fact the bordering areas weren't just states, but different countries all together. The gendarmerie waved us through without stopping the car. The BASE-Duvel team was heading off for the Normandy region in northern France for a UCI 1.12 race. This was to be my thirty-sixth race since I had arrived in Belgium.

The last two months after my first UCI race were occupied full of uneventful events. The BASE-Duvel team was racing more than I cared to keep track and I was into a daily, monotonous routine of eat, sleep, and ride or race my bike. I stopped almost all training, as the races around Gent were so plentiful all I was doing was racing, recovering, then racing again.

The races were all hard and were all good for me, but not one was filled with any great, distinguishing moments. I had hit a plateau in my development, with no noticeable improvements seen. I was finishing most all of my races, but when the winning moves happened I wasn't able to hang on. I never felt truly fatigued and I never felt truly fresh. I was in a perpetual state of mediocrity, riding on a Möbius strip of muted results.

The other guys in the house were on highs and lows. After his stellar performance in Hasselt, Troy found his legs for a good month-long period of time. He was always up in the top twenty of any climbing race and cracked the top ten in two Kermesse races. Ken and Sergei both cracked the top five in several Kermesse races. Ken also had a highlight of making an extremely long one hundred and fifty kilometer breakaway in a UCI race, only to have the break caught in the final five kilometers of the race. He was disappointed, but it was a good showing of pure power. The sporadically high points aside, the general consensus as of late has been more lows than highs.

The best part of the last week has definitely been the Tour de France on TV. The Tour's coverage has been amazing. I have had a choice of four different languages—Dutch, French, German, and Spanish—in which to watch the race, and the coverage was for four hours every day, uninterrupted. My usual routine on days when I wasn't racing was to plan out my day so that I would finish my day's ride around two in the afternoon. When I got back to the apartment I would be able to relax lazily in front of the TV for two to three hours, enjoying the action of the Tour unfolding.

Today I would rather be watching the Tour than doing this race, but Peter needed riders to come, as they were paying good money to have teams show up. It was a chance to be guaranteed some money just from starting.

We arrived in the small French villa of Parenty after getting a little lost. It was a standard problem when finding the little towns, and

Peter and the team planned accordingly with a departure time that allotted for "being lost time." The race was to be a 140-kilometer race over fourteen laps of ten kilometers, so basically an oversized Kermesse. Parenty was a beautiful little villa with a large cathedral and matching town hall, with the central square kept pristinely clean accenting its intricately laid brickwork.

I lingered out of the car and started to stretch my legs from the drive. I was getting spoiled living in Belgium, as any drive of over any hour to a race seemed to be so far away. I could remember not even using a moment's worth of debate in driving five to six hours to do an hour criterium back in the U.S. I don't know how I could go back to the U.S. and do the racing circuit like I did before after the system in Europe.

Peter went with Danny to find the team meeting and the rest of us put out some chairs under the shade of a large oak tree and enjoyed the French scenery. The team was a full squad of eight riders: four Belgians and everyone from the apartment. The Belgian riders on the team had been getting a bit apprehensive with the guys in the house because our results had resulted in selection for UCI races. For my part I just ignored the problem and the other riders, preferring to expend my energies on uprooting myself out of my results rut.

I watched Peter walk over toward us with a look of frustration upon his face.

He came over and started to explain, "Well, guys, the faxed confirmation they sent me said we had a team meeting at ten a.m.; it's actually at eleven a.m., and the start of the race isn't till one p.m., not noon. I talked to another team director who is also here early and he told me this is the sponsoring club's first time putting on this race. So I should have expected some problems."

I was a little glad for the delay, as I had slept terribly the last two nights and needed a little nap to get some extra energy. I pulled my towel out of my bag, laid it down on the grass under the shade of the tree, and put my backpack under my head. I propped my feet up on my chair and let my eyelids rest heavily.

The next thing I knew I felt a gentle wetness fall on my head. It happened again and I opened my eyes to see Ken and Sergei standing over me with a water bottle slowly dripping water. Ken started off.

"Wake up, sleepy head, gotta get ready for the race."

I looked up at him.

"How long do we have till the start of the race?"

"About forty-five minutes, but it's France, so you really never know."

I got up and collected my things and looked around to see that much time had passed since I fell asleep. There were riders and team cars everywhere, and people were filling the town square for the start of the race. I looked at my watch to see that I had fallen asleep for almost two hours. I felt better but my body longed for more sleep. I hurried to catch up with Sergei and Ken as they went in search of the dressing rooms.

At the team meeting, Peter went over the race course, a flat circuit with a few corners in it. The main concern he had was the mention of some roundabouts and medians throughout the course.

Peter went on to explain, "You guys gotta keep your eyes open out there. The medians in the region can be a big danger. They are low to the ground and are not well marked."

He continued and pointed out the other good teams and who to mark on their teams. I took mental note of the riders and their respective numbers and dispersed with the rest of the team to warm up for the race.

I arrived at the start line ten minutes before the scheduled start, but I couldn't find one official in sight. I found Troy and asked him but he just shrugged his shoulders, so I went looking for the big boss to get the lowdown on the situation. I found Peter coming out of the town hall again with the look of disappointment on his face.

He started off solemnly, "It seems the course isn't secured yet; the officials are out there right now with the organizers getting things straightened out. The race has been delayed by one hour. Go spread the word to the guys when you see them."

I found most of the guys on the start line in a state of confusion. I let them know the situation and we all went back to the team cars to get some water and find some shade. We waited out the hour in a small café crammed with riders watching the Tour de France on television.

Some of the locals came over to me but all I could do was smile and nod.

They would ramble on for about two minutes then asked me in French, "*Parlez-vous français?*"

I stupidly replied, "*Un peu,*" or "a little," to the first to ask.

They took this to mean I knew half of the hundred-thousand-word vocabulary of French and started to ramble on and on. After many problems, I finally got one of the Belgian guys to come over and explain to them that I didn't speak French.

At two o'clock, we gathered at the start area, and there were officials present, but there was an announcement of an additional delay of fifteen minutes. I was beginning to suspect I was going to spend more time in my chamois today just sitting around than I was actually racing my bike at this rate. I found myself a nice shaded spot by the start line under the officials' canopy. I wasn't going to wait out in the sun.

Finally, the start of the race came and the officials went on in a lengthy talk that my teammate told me was nothing more than "useless bullcrap talk," as he misquoted the slang saying. The starting gun went off, and as quickly as the speed went up so did my heart rate. I felt the pounding beat of my heart reverberate in my chest, and my breaths were abrupt and cursory as we accelerated out of the town.

The riders at the front of the race were blazing the speed from the start, and my legs were cold after the long delay and were not happy to be going so hard so quickly. I pressed on and focused on maintaining contact with the wheel in front of me. The effort just to hold onto the wheel in front of me was almost too much for me. After the first lap, I couldn't believe that I had thirteen equivalent laps to look forward to.

On the second lap, I could feel my heart rate spike into the unbelievably uncomfortable zones with each attack. I watched Ken follow an attack up the road and I couldn't even think about jumping onto his wheel. Then a strange thing happened. I watched one of the Belgian teammates go up to the front of the race and start to pull back the break that Ken had just made. I couldn't believe what I was seeing, as it is a mutiny and an extreme travesty to pull such an action against a teammate. If I had the strength to, I would have gone up there to stop it from happening. But I couldn't.

Between watching the sabotage at the front and the pain of just trying to hold on, I wasn't paying attention too well to what was happening. I looked forward to notice two riders in front of me quickly move to the right. I knew the instant I saw the movement, and my internal reaction made me pull heavily upward on my handlebars. I felt my front wheel clear but my reaction wasn't good enough to save my rear wheel from hitting. The center median hit hard and the rear wheel was bounced up into the air. All I could think, while briefly suspended in midair, was that I didn't break anything or have a flat. I landed hard but unscathed. These were the moments my winters of cyclocross came in extremely handy.

My attention came full circle with the impact, but did nothing to help me lower my heart rate with an additional amount of adrenaline coursing through my veins. Ken's breakaway was pulled back by the end of lap two and leading into lap three, where things went from bad to detrimental. I felt the pain in my legs start to hurt beyond my tolerance threshold, then a little more, and then I just couldn't take it. I just had to stop to relieve the pain, as it was too much to endure. I faded off the back of the group and through the caravan. On the way back I looked up at Peter in the caravan with dejected eyes, moving my head side to side in remorse for my pathetic performance.

I was dead. I was beyond dead. In fact, death would have been sweet surrender compared to this state. I kept rolling along at a snail's pace all the way to the feed zone, where I went over to the side of the road and just sat there. I sat on the roadside curb, drinking my water bottle, muttering to myself in self-pity about my inability to perform. I was looking at the ground in front of me when a pair of feet appeared in my space for staring. I looked up to see a man smiling an impish grin at me.

I glared a look at him and asked roughly, "Can I help you?"

He didn't say anything for a moment then started, "Are you an American?"

"Yeah."

"Oh, okay ... so was it a hard race?"

"Yeah, I'm having a shit day. I hate when these days happen."

"Well, European racing can be very hard. The racing here is long and fast. You know, here in Europe all the riders prepare a little differently than they do in the U.S." He reached in his shirt pocket and pulled out a business card. "I am a doctor and I have many successful clients who I help prepare for racing in Europe. Maybe you give me a call?"

I looked at the card; it only had a name and a phone number, nothing else. I put it in my back pocket and said nothing else to him. He walked off and I was glad. Once he left, I took the card out and crumbled it up, casting it into the street in front of me. There was no way

I was going to get involved with whatever crap that glorified snake oil salesman had to offer. The price of my life wasn't worth the performance benefit, much less the ethics of it all.

I rolled back to the team cars, got my bag out, and found the showers to clean up. When I returned from the *vestiaires*, I found four more of the Base-Duvel riders by the team cars, including Sergei and Troy. At the end of the race, the team only had Ken and one other rider finish the race, and neither was in a placing worthy of note.

When Peter arrived at the team cars, I could see the look of disappointment highlighted with lines of anger on his face. He walked over with determined direction and boldly stated.

"Everyone, gather round for a team meeting. This will be short. First off, I am very disappointed in how this team is racing. I have been informed by other team directors that you all were chasing each other down during the race. This is unacceptable and won't happen again! If it does happen again, there won't be a next time for you to screw up. Now second, I have been watching all of the riders for the past two weeks and most everyone is performing under their best levels. You all have been racing full tilt for almost three months now and it's time for a break. This next week in Gent is the annual *Gentse Feesten,* so I have decided to let everyone on the team have a deserved and needed ten-day break from racing. You can ride your bike if you like, but I don't suggest anything over an hour. This is time to recuperate and take your mind off cycling. Go out and have fun. That's all I have to say."

I had never seen Peter with such harshness in his voice; his normally subtle nature was inflamed into not quite anger but utter annoyance. I didn't question his decision. Hell, I was thankful for it. I was relieved to have time to decompress from the monotony that had engulfed my days. I was on the brink of mental collapse and I was thrown a tether to pull me from the edge and onto the safety of a solid foundation.

VI—Incessant Inner Fire

My body's internal metronome awoke me at my usual 7:30, but today I didn't arise. In fact, I went right back down onto my pillow, threw the covers over my head, and headed back into the wonderful world of dreams. I didn't return to the realm of reality for another three hours. I totaled almost twelve hours of sleep that night. My body needed more than rest than I had originally anticipated.

I went into the living room and plopped myself lethargically into the deep crevices of the worn-out couch. The TV didn't provide much entertainment for me. There wasn't much programming on in English. I started to get excited seeing one of my favorite cartoons, *Dextor's Laboratory*, come on the TV only to be disappointed when I started to hear Dextor talk in Dutch. Still it was entertaining for about all of five minutes before I flipped through the channels again but still found nothing.

No one was around. I knew Troy was already up, but I didn't know where he was and I hadn't seen Ken or Sergei. It felt weird having no plan to my day. Every day since I arrived had a purpose to it and I knew my task in cycling to be accomplished that day. But today there was no set task, nothing to accomplish, no preparing or recovery, nothing to do. So that is what I decided to do: nothing.

Just as I decided doing nothing was the something I would be doing, my stomach started to grumble with the sounds of hunger. I started to walk toward the pantry for my customary bowl of Muesli, but then I stopped. Today and the nine days to follow weren't about health and fitness; they were about fun and debauchery. A venting of compounded and confined pleasures that the athlete denies himself in his sacrifice for his love of the sport. I turned about-face and headed out the door. It was time to visit the wonderful land of pastries and treats known as the bakery.

For almost five months I walked into the bakery every couple of days for my bread and I stared at all the wondrous treats and sugary concoctions under the glass case while I stood in line. I didn't deny myself the occasional treat, but I certainly would have liked to consume more than the occasional pastry. Today I walked in with a nice little grin on my face. Self-denial of pleasure was exiled and I listened to the little red-suited friend perched upon my shoulder today.

I greeted the young woman, whose name I now knew was Annika, with the customary *"oe'ist"* slang greeting particular to Flanders. She greeted me with a smile but still replied back in English. The shopkeepers of the stores I frequented all knew me by name and were always interested to know how I and the other guys in the house were doing with cycling and life. We were sort of local celebrities to some of the people of the neighborhood.

Today I was getting the one treat that always hit the spot and was even appropriate for the semi-breakfast I was emulating. I smiled and started off, "Annika, I would like four *pannekoeken* and two *chocoladekoeken*." The *pannekoeken* were Belgian versions of crepes and were great heated up with a little chocolate spread. Both were typical breakfast items in Belgium, but not for consumption daily.

I walked around the neighborhood snacking on my sweet breakfast delights enjoying the cool, brisk wind. Summertime was rather pleasant in Belgium. Being so far north in latitude, the temperatures rarely exceeded the mid-nineties, and upper eighties typified the summer months. Gent was bustling with people. There were students everywhere with the summer vacation well under way, tourists abounded, and there were workers all around setting up tents all over the city for Gentse Feesten. I hadn't seen so many kegs of beer just lying around ever in my entire life.

I meandered my way over to a bookshop near the center of town that carried English-print magazines and more specifically carried *CycleSport*. I went in, browsed through several magazines to kill some time, and then searched a little while to find the latest *CycleSport*. With reading material in hand, I made my way to the shadow of the Belfry to a little café I frequented.

Ken showed me the little café one day on a rest day during my first month in Gent. He liked it because it was just off the beaten path, but still had enough people that walked by to make for some good people watching. De Eeuwige Bron was a quaint little two-story coffee shop owned by a pleasant elderly couple, Henreette and Jean-Pierre. I sat down and ordered a coffee to quench the growing caffeine craving brewing in my body.

I started at the beginning of the *CycleSport* and worked all the way to the end, consuming four more cups of coffee, albeit typically small, European-sized ones, and a *Croque Monsieur gegratineerd met kaas*. The Croque Monsieur is a grilled cheese and ham sandwich placed in a bowl, covered in a heavy cream sauce, and topped with cheese. It's then baked and the cheese is browned. Health points score a zero but taste points score a one hundred. I used up all the afternoon and was working on the beginning of the evening by the time I was finished. I started back for the apartment as the orange hue of the setting sun glistened against the buildings.

I walked inside the apartment to the pleasant aroma and sound of searing meat. Ken was behind the stove cooking up one of his famous dinners. He would pull intricate recipes off the Internet and spend a couple of hours preparing them. He said he did it to kill time, because when you are cooking you're not eating. I would help out when I felt up to the challenge and I had been learning some really cool cooking techniques, but more often than not I would relegate myself to cleanup duties in exchange for a portion of the day's tasty creation.

Ken greeted me as I walked into the kitchen, "How ya doin', mate?"

"Just fine ... relaxed!"

"That's good, so what you been up to today?"

"Well, to quote one of my favorite movies, *Office Space*, 'Today I did nothing and it was everything I thought it could be.'"

"Sounds like a ripe old time ... Andy, you want in on the dinner? I have some steaks that were going to be going bad, so I am cooking them all now. There's also some salad and some sautéed potatoes."

"Yeah, man, that would be perfect, as I didn't have much of anything planned."

"Okay, standard drill: I cook, you clean?"

"Fine by me!"

I helped prepare the table and we sat down to enjoy a wonderful meal.

As I was finishing up cleaning, Ken made a suggestion.

"Hey, Andy, how about we grab Troy and Sergei and go downstairs to t'Kleintje. We can do a bit more of the nothing by consuming a plethora of empty calories."

I raised an eyebrow.

"Ken, you read my mind! Let's do it."

Troy took a fair of amount of prodding, but after a bit of guilt-tripping I got him away from his book and we joined Sergei and Ken downstairs.

t'Kleintje was well known for its many varieties of beers, over two hundred, and that night we set out on the task of trying each and every one of them. Unfortunately, we didn't succeed, but we had a grand old time, and without the ominous pressure of performing at a forthcoming race, we were all relaxed. It was the first time in four months we all really went out and just hung out late into the night as friends, not teammates.

It was also that night I remembered something Ken had told me the first day: there were seventy steps from the bar to the apartment. I happened to remember this idle fact about halfway up the stairs on my crawl back to my bed, but I had assistance from Sergei, who helped me in my ascent to the front door. Troy, in keeping with expectations of his abilities as a climber, won the King of the Drunken Stairs Ascent. For a small guy, he could hold his liquor with the best of them. I made it to my bed after a long crawl and drifted into slumber as I tried to ignore the spinning of the ceiling.

* * *

I arose from my bed with the feeling that someone was knocking bricks against the sides of my head. The unpleasantness wasn't reserved for just me, as I found Ken laying half on the couch and half on the floor. I wanted the banging to stop, so I brewed up some coffee and took two Dafalgan to help make my head feel slightly smaller. I changed into some fresh clothes and wandered my way down to the bakery to get a few pannekoeken.

I couldn't remember the last time I went out and had so much to drink. The sporting side of the night's activities wasn't very beneficial, but the mental side of it was advantageous. I needed a night like that to free myself from the pressures and stress I'd been feeling in my idle state of performance.

Back at the apartment, Ken was awake and inhaling a large cup of coffee, while Troy was up and about with a skippy disposition that contradicted the sheer amount of beverage he had consumed the previous night. It was just past noon and we all gathered around the TV to watch the start of that day's extended coverage for the Tour stage in the Alps. The coverage was exciting and we used the downtime to recover from our drinking efforts.

Toward the latter part of the stage they showed an animated map of the day's route and the distance already covered. Shortly they transitioned into another animation of the next day's stage, a mountain time trial up L'Alpe d'Huez. We all started debating the challenges of such a hard effort and who was going to run the best chance of winning the stage.

In the middle of it all Troy said, "Man, it would be so cool to go watch that stage. To see the suffering on the faces of all the riders."

Something in my head just clicked and I looked over at Troy. He stared back at me and grinned at the unspoken words we both knew. Simultaneously, we both jumped up and ran over to the computer and started to click away at the Internet. After some short bits of sleuthing, we figured we could make it to Brussels before the last Thalys high-speed train left, bound for Grenoble and arrive late in the night. We would find a hostel for the night and then wake up in the morning and find a way to L'Alpe d'Huez.

Ken looked at us in disbelief. We tried to persuade him to come, but he said he preferred to stay at the apartment and just enjoy the stage from the comfort of the couch. Sergei wanted to go but said he didn't have the money. So Troy and I quickly packed a small backpack each with some essentials and headed for the train station.

We made the train to Brussels in comfortable time to make the connection for the Thalys to Grenoble. From there it would be a trip of five hours, where we would rest up and catch the little sleep we would receive in the next days. I found my seat but could hardly keep still. In less than twenty-four hours, I would be on the slopes of one of the most infamous climbs of cycling's most prestigious race during its pinnacle stage. The proximity and accessibility in Europe amazed me. I could have never pulled off something like this off in the U.S. without a car, there is just no logistical way to make it happen. I put my bag away and set my seat back as I relaxed and tried to drift into a slight slumber.

* * *

"Andy, we are there … Andy?"

I heard the voice but didn't want to open my eyes. I wanted to hit the snooze button, but conscious realization of where I was took hold and I forced myself to arise. Troy stood in front of me with my backpack in hand. I grabbed it and we headed off the train and onto the platform. Half asleep and using the world's worse French, Troy and I eventually found the hostel.

Troy and I checked out of the hostel early in the morning. We wanted to stake out our spot as soon as possible. I was sure that there are many people who were already camped out all along the climb.

Troy asked me, "Well, what now?"

"I'm not quite sure; give me a second."

We were so close, only fifteen kilometers away, but still so far. We couldn't walk the distance to the start and we had to find some way to get there. I then noticed a person walking by with a yellow cap. It was embossed with the Tour de France logo. I produced a plan.

"Troy, look for people with some sort of yellow hat or T-shirt. In this whole town there has to be someone who is going to the race and is willing to give us a ride."

I really thought this was going to be a tough pitch to pull, but it was surprisingly quite easy. Only five minutes into our search, we found a couple, Dianne and Tom from Atlanta, Georgia, eating brunch outside a café. Tom and Dianne were both recreational riders who had started cycling late in their lives after Tom had problems with his knees from running. They had a rental car with some extra room and were more than happy to give us a lift. They even invited us to join them for brunch. They bombarded us with questions about what two young Americans were doing in Europe, and Troy and I went into the whole narrative about how we were in Belgium to race and our off-the-wall decision to come see the stage.

After brunch, we all piled into a typical European-sized car that would only pass as a subcompact in the U.S., but I wasn't going to complain, as we had a ride to the race start. The arrival at the start was breathtaking. A massive maze of semi-trucks and cars all parked at the bottom of the climb. It was a little village that was assembled and disassembled each day and moved to its new location. I had seen photos, heard stories, and watched tapes of the race, but nothing could compare to physically experiencing firsthand the reality of the amazing complexity of the Tour. Troy and I couldn't be kept from grinning, and our heads were moving back in forth in all directions to try and visually consume it all.

At this point, we thanked Tom and Dianne and let them go their own way. They left us with an open offer of a ride back if we could find them. We had plans to go most of the way up the climb, while they were going to stay in the starting area. Troy and I began our ascent by foot up the steep L'Alpe d'Huez.

After fifteen minutes, my feet began to ache. Here I was, a fit athlete crippled by the simple act of walking. A cyclist's legs weren't meant for these motions; I would have been better off on a bike. The warm air moved very little in the protection of the mountain, and beads of sweat formed on my brow in rapid production. It was going to be a hard but fast day on the climb for the riders with the heated air.

After a kilometer, we found a small Peugeot going up the climb and hitched a ride on the back bumper while it puttered along up the climb. We rode on the back for about six kilometers till we found a corner with a vista view to watch the race. It was perfect because we would be able to watch the riders come by once, then run up the side of the mountain to catch a second glimpse, if we so desired. The location also allowed us to watch about one kilometer of the ascent below us and a few hundred meters of the climb above us. We parked ourselves into a nice spot and lay down on the side of the slope to rest from all the travel.

While lying back enjoying the beautiful day, we started to hear some people speaking English next to us and decided to introduce ourselves. The introduction wasn't purely social as we also noticed they had a TV hooked up to their camper RV. Once again we received an open and warm reception. The owners of the RV were an English family, the Allens, from Harrow near London. The Allens weren't even avid cyclists, but just wanted to see the Tour on their "holiday" in southern France. Apparently, no one in England uses the word vacation, as it is a Yankee term. Troy and I went through our whole story of our situation and how these two Americans came about being in the middle of nowhere in France.

As we waited for the start of the riders, we were treated to the parade of cars that preceded each of the Tour's stages, where sponsors would throw trinkets and samples to the fans. I was able to score a key chain from Aquarel and two large plastic tubes from PMU that you bang together to make a loud sound.

The first of the riders could be seen far below starting the ascent. The riders were the last ones on GC and had no chance at the Maillot Jaune, but that didn't stop the fans from still cheering them on in relentless jubilance. I would have suspected the cheering to subside after the first twenty or so riders, but it stayed at a steady roar consistently throughout the mountain time trial; of course, there was your occasional extreme outburst from the crowd for a favored French rider. After four hours of riders going by, the last ten riders started the ascent and the crowd became alive in a fury of passionate vigor. These were the riders who had real chances at the Maillot Jaune, and their faces showed lines of determination accented with clinched teeth and beads of perspiration.

Each one for them was in the zone—a place where time and reality have no control over the mind. The mind looks at reality through the lens of perception to alter the truth into a rational sense it can handle. Riders turn the pain inward and manipulate the subconscious sensory of malice the body is sending to the brain into perceived senses of pleasure. It was elegance in motion to view the pure climbers ascend the steep gradients. They danced upon the pedals with seemingly effortless motion with each stroke of the leg.

Troy and I crowded the road with the other fans as the final riders started to make their way to the top. I was one of those many nameless fans I had seen on TV shaking their hands and clapping in delight at the riders while gendarmerie honked to clear a way for the riders. I sensed the hairs stand up on the back of my neck as reality of the experience became conscious.

Then the pinnacle of the crowd's enthusiasm was reached as the glistening yellow jersey of the Maillot Jaune ascended the climb. Seeing the yellow fibers of the jersey in the tangible reality of sight only mere feet away from my eyes was so sensational the truth was made to feel fictitious. I watched as the leader of the Tour climbed his way through the hordes of screaming fans. I watched each bead of sweat drip from his brow, laced with a capacious array of veins beating blood throughout his body to recuperate the fatigue of the effort. Each muscle in his arms and legs was distinctively defined with the strain of each pedal stroke over his thin, tan epidermis. His eyes showed the look of an animal in the throws of battle; keen sharp movements and concentration marked his face. He was encompassed in the zone, readily pushing his body beyond the limits imposed by the mind and to the brink of bodily extremes. The look of a champion embodied his face, a man who knows the path before him, knew how to distance the path, and finally knows he can achieve the length of the path. Seeing him engulfed in the zone with this disposition, I knew he was going to go on to win the Tour. There was no doubt in my mind.

Troy and I looked over at each other after the Maillot Jaune left our sight. We both were jumping up and down in excitement and quickly rushed back over to the RV to watch the rest of the ascent to the top of the climb. The Maillot Jaune kept up with his role as the leader and dominated the time trial, a full minute faster than even the specialist climbers.

As the race was over, a mass exodus of fans, team support, and riders started for the bottom of the hill. Troy and I found relief from walking by means of a sponsor vehicle, a giant coffee cup from Grande Mere, which we hitched a ride on the side of to the bottom of the climb. At the bottom, we tried in vain to find Dianne and Tom but had little luck. We ended up hitching a ride with a German guy back to Grenoble. We found the first train back to Brussels and headed on our return trip to home for a late-night arrival. We walked into the apartment shattered with weariness and we both headed directly to our beds.

* * *

I emerged from my room the next morning after ten hours of solid slumber. The past few days of intense travel had taken a toll on my body, which I was paying for in discomfort and weariness. I shuffled my feet along lethargically through the living room as I was greeted by Ken.

"Top o' the morning to ya, Mr. Superstar!"

I crinkled my eyebrows together in curiosity to the interesting choice in greeting.

"What you talking about?"

"You and Troy were on TV yesterday. It was only a few seconds, but we saw you guys on the climb."

How cool was that. We made it on TV!

I started off in the best aristocratic, Hollywood tone I could muster at such a dreadfully early morning hour, "Really … well, no autographs before my morning coffee. Call my agent to set up an appointment."

I grabbed my customary morning cup of coffee and headed to the computer to peruse my usual set of cycling news sites for a daily dose of gossip served with a side of truth.

Ken yelled over to me from the kitchen table, "Hey Andy, you want to go to Gentse Feesten tonight?"

"Sure, I am totally down for some more drinking debauchery."

"Good 'cause I invited some of the other BASE-Duvel riders."

I turned around in my chair with a confused look on my face.

"You did what …? Why?"

Ken started off in a steady and stern tone, "'Cause someone needed to do it … we have placed ourselves in a situation where we are in their country, on their team, and living away from them. They don't know us, and it creates an Us-versus-Them situation. That is why things perpetuated to the level of dysfunction we saw at the last race. At first we weren't a threat, but with some decent results we are taking spots in high-profile UCI races they feel should go to them. Do you see where I am going with this?"

"Yeah, but they are the reason for the problem; it's not being perpetuated by us."

"Do you think they will just up and decide one day, without knowing us, to start respecting us? No. So we need to extend a hand in friendship first."

"I guess it makes sense. I mean, I don't like the guys on the team … but I don't dislike them either."

"And why is that?"

"'Cause I don't know them. …'"

I paused and rolled my eyes upward in personal reflection of my stupidity. I walked head-on into my own answer. I went back to my Internet surfing and didn't give much extra thought to the situation.

Later that night we met four other riders from the team. Two of them, Tim and Jan, were Beloften, under twenty-three riders, whom we didn't race with that much and I didn't know. The other two, Bijorn De Weaver and Peter Hagers, were riders I knew, but didn't know. Each of them had raced with us in France last week, and I didn't know if they were the ones who chased down any of the guys from the house.

The lot of us started off near the Gravensteen Castle, where there was a band, Janez Debt, playing punk music, and in English no less. I asked Bijorn if the group was from America or England, but as it turned out they were Belgian. I couldn't understand why they would sing in English and Ken clarified the point for me.

"Think about it, Andy: most people here speak English and almost all the music on the radio is already in English, so English is a natural choice. Also if you sing in any language other than English you get classified under 'World Music.' This way a band can get their music to a much larger audience and sell it easier."

It all made sense to me and I accepted it at face value.

The crowd was dense and I would have guessed a third of Belgium was in Gent for the night's festival. We wandered through the crowd before finally settling down near the veranda of a café. I leaned against the short, wrought iron fencing to alleviate the pressure on my legs, as I have a distinct disdain for standing. We talked about cycling and asked the guys about how they had started in cycling. I was amazed to learn about how much cycling was accessible and available to a young child in Belgium. It was similar to little league baseball back in the U.S., wherein local community groups would organize group rides and even sometimes provided equipment. They would learn skills drills early in their development and the Kermesse-style racing started as young as ten years old. No wonder these riders were hardened veterans of cycling in their early twenties.

As the conversation continued, Bijorn and I shifted into our own personal conversation. I was telling him about my long winter of training with Jurgen and how much my parents disapproved of what I was doing. He seemed a bit surprised by my enthusiasm.

"You have a real passion for the bike. You went against your parents and came to a foreign land for cycling. That must have been hard."

"It was, but it wasn't. Inside of me, I knew this was something I needed to do. It was a necessity of life, like breathing or eating. So coming here wasn't as hard as one might think. I actually really enjoy living in Belgium. What has been hard is adapting to the racing and learning to suffer on a totally new level."

I noticed Bijorn look over my right shoulder and then nod in the same direction. I glanced over to see a group of girls at a table giggling with laughter.

"Andy, that girl has been staring in your direction now for ten minutes. You need to talk to her."

Ken overheard the conversation and interjected, "A girl, aye? Looks like the prospect is agreeable to a linguistic interaction. Go talk to her, mate."

"Yeah, but what do I say ...? I mean, I don't speak Dutch."

Bijorn said, "Tell her, *'Je hebt een schoon kontje.'* It means, 'You have beautiful eyes.' It's local slang."

I noticed Ken chuckle a little.

I started off, "Okay, I'll do it ... just need a bit of the old confidence booster."

I held up the rest of my beer up and downed the remainder of my glass in one swift motion. I breathed in a deep, controlled breath and exhaled the nervous feelings running down my spine. I pulled on a large, smiling grin and walked over to the girl confidently. She was seated with several other girls, which didn't make my task any easier, but her deep emerald eyes compelled me into conversation.

I repeated the phrase again in my head and confidently conversed, "Hello ... *Je hebt een schoon koentje!*"

I watched her elegant lips straighten as her eyes narrowed. I heard an uproar of laugher from behind me and glanced back to see the guys almost in tears at my compelling situation. I instantaneously realized I hadn't said my intended meaning. I looked back to the girl, who was still in slight shock at my words.

Boldly and not missing a beat I said, "Well, it seems there has been a bit of confusion in what I have said. I just wanted to tell you that your eyes are enchantingly beautiful. ... Now, may I inquire as to what I actually said?"

The girl smiled gently and giggled, "You told me I have a nice butt."

"Really? Well, it seems I have been played a fool by my teammates, but it is of little concern to me as it was a good way to meet a beautiful woman like yourself."

I glanced back at the group, who were now all staring in my direction blankly. I suspect they thought I would fail miserably, but to the group's surprise, I was triumphant.

I continued, "My name is Andy Bennet. It is an extreme pleasure to meet you."

She blushed and said, "My name is Sofie."

We talked for a good ten minutes and conversed in the typical banter each person goes through with the opposite sex upon first meeting. I then took a chance.

"You know what …? You have many lovely friends; perhaps they would like to meet my teammates?"

Sofie said, "Well, okay."

We all walked over to the guys and I played host introducing everyone in the group to the group of girls. The rest of the night we all socialized to the wee hours of the morning, enjoying each other's company. In the middle of it all Bijorn leaned over to me.

"You have balls, Andy … big balls."

I laughed and Sofie asked me what it was I found so funny. I excused the laughter as typical guy stuff she would not understand. The night continued on to the rise of a new day.

* * *

Vacation went by faster than anticipated. Before I knew it, the days of Gentse Feesten were behind me and I was back on the bike. I started to feel the need and lust for the bike around day seven of my vacation. It was a weird feeling to wake up and not have to be riding a bike, so my return to the bike was a needed relief from the feelings of withdrawal I was experiencing. My first two days back on the bike were very easy, each ride just two hours long, and simple spins along the Schelde to Oudenaarde for some coffee.

I sat on the couch with my morning coffee, debating where I wanted to ride. I picked up a map of Belgium off the end table and began running my finger in a zigzag motion across the surface. My eyes tracked roads leading to and from Gent while my finger followed the visual path. I traced a satisfying path toward the southwest to include some nice hills with flat sections and I readied myself for the ride. Walking outside to the garage, the warm breeze of heated summer air brushed its way through my hair as I descended the stairs. The crystal blue oasis of sky was without a solitary cloud, and illuminating, intense rays of sun cast clear, precise shadows. I prepared my bike and stuffed some extra tubes into my back jersey pockets for some extra insurance during my ride.

Leaving Gent I noticed the warm weather brought out an astounding number of people for a weekday at ten in the morning. People filled all the verandas and patios of almost every café I passed. I couldn't imagine all these people didn't have to be at work, but then again Europe tends to become very relaxed in the summer. Harsh winters and generally rainy springs and falls bring most Belgians outside when it is sunny. I too wasn't planning on wasting such a splendid summer day inside and would enjoy every minute of the ride.

I rolled down the Schelde with a gingerly rhythm, navigating my way through the traffic of recreational riders along the trail. There is nothing more vexing to my mind, or reassuring to Belgium's cycling obsession, than to witness a group of twenty-some-odd elderly ladies dressed in typical clothing, riding two abreast in a double paceline. The little old ladies were holding a line better than half the category four riders I knew and probably rode an echelon better at that, albeit all at the incredible speed of fifteen kilometers per hour. Once I got to Oudenaarde, I headed west to Anzegem and continued on to Kortrijk. I arrived in Kortrijk and located a bakery to get a refill of water and buy some broodpudding, the cheapest, most calorie-intense, halfway-healthy ride food in Belgium. Locating a bakery in Belgium is like finding south when you are at the North Pole: just look in any direction and you're going to find one. Whether or not they were open was a different matter. I located a bakery with ease on the main road just as I started to arrive in town.

I stepped out of the bakery into the warmth of the sunlight feeling the gentle breeze again roll across my face. My original plan was to head to the north and work my way up to the Brugge-Gent canal and then head home, but I wanted to continue my ride and not waste this glorious summer weather. I pulled out my map and looked for a new route and direction to take. I searched across the map till a name popped out at me: Kemmel. I wanted to go there.

The Kemmelberg is one of the few famous cobbled climbs I hadn't done since I arrived in Belgium. It is located almost one hundred kilometers away from Gent, so riding to there would be quite a long day in the saddle. Today, however, I was thirsty to quench my lust for riding after my ten-day hiatus from my two-wheeled friend. It was time to place some strain upon the muscles and let them reawaken to the pleasure of pain.

Rejuvenated, I hopped on my bike and headed to the west, meandering my way through the long back roads of Belgium. The roads were small, desolate, and perfect for losing yourself in the Zen rhythm of consistent pace pushing. I rolled along the roads with expedited speed, driving my heart rate up into the zone just below my threshold limit, but above my level of comfort.

The rolling roads traversed extensive distances of fields speckled with intermittent trees as my tires thumped to the gentle rhythm of the concrete separations while I rolled along in my self-imposed state of discomfort. These were the moments I loved most in the world: a man and his bike … alone, free, and uninhibited. Time when the worries of the world are sweated out from your insides and evaporate in the great expanse of the road you leave in your wake. The town-to-town directional path of my trip flowed in a blur of time whose reality was not congruent to the perception.

I approached the foot of the Kemmelberg with an inner desire to conquer the hill. I felt the pressure and strain increase against my feet as I started the beginning of the incline to the top and pushed myself harder against the demon of the hill. The internal combustion of elements started to seep out the waste, and the muscles screamed out for relief from the pressure. I ignored the brain's internal warning system of pain and clinched my teeth to alleviate the pain. I turned the left-hand corner and started the ascent of the cobbled section.

This is when I started to really feel the burn. I glanced down at my heart rate monitor and saw my heart rate at 203 beats per minute, one beat over maximum. My brain wanted to accept this as my pinnacle of pain, but I wouldn't let the Kemmel conquer me. I shifted up one gear, tightened my grip on the handlebars, and stood up to push myself all the way to the top. I was in a level of pain I had never felt before; my arteries pumped full, hard, pulsing beats to counteract the pain as my breathing increased to the edge of physical limits.

I crested the top of the climb and felt the jarring of the cobbles cease. My mind started to return to the realm of reality as I heard the sounds of clapping in the background. I drew a short glance to my side to see a small group of people cheering me on in my self-sadistic ascent of personal self-discovery. The bike was my way of testing myself, seeing my personal limits, then trying to exceed them. It's exciting when you surprise others, but to surprise yourself by exceeding your own personally thought limits, that is utterly thrilling to the soul.

I stopped my pedaling and coasted my way over to the left side of the road. I unclipped a foot and firmly planted it on the ground, but it faltered from the fatigue still consuming my bodily fibers and I came crashing down to the ground with a large thud. I just lay there on the ground for a couple of minutes, staring up at the towering tribute to the fallen warriors of the World Wars. Once I gathered the energy, I arose from the ground and dusted myself off. I looked back at the road I had just conquered and drew and long, slender grin across my face. I went beyond the realm of my known reality.

I mounted my bike and descended the dangerous backside of the Kemmelberg. I pedaled along on my way home and I let my mind wander back into a state of conscious realization. I started to contemplate why I loved the bike. I was passing along a desolate back road when a revelation crossed from the subconscious to the conscious reality of life.

To me cycling was not just about a person on a two-wheeled machine. It's a venue through which man is able to manifest life … the passion, the glory, the failure. The drive and passion of man is transformed from the metaphysical to the physical through the sweat and pain of each pedal stroke. … A man has never lived till he has mentally died upon a bike. … He is reborn anew; the lifting of the veil of pain shows him a clearer vision of life because he has seen the other side. Only when a man has known this dichotomy of the sides of life will he understand life. The cyclist is a special breed privy to this knowledge because his bike is the gap between these two parts of life's reality. A cyclist not only knows life's existence, he exists in the knowledge of life.

I felt the back of my neck tingle at the thoughts I had running through my head. I knew now my attraction and obsession of the bike. It was more than a vehicle for transportation; it was a venue through which I was able to see and live my life. The rest of the ride I spent in a daze, soaking in the knowledge I had just accrued. I arrived back home at the apartment after seven hours and two hundred kilometers of riding. I was physically exhausted to the point of collapse, but I had never been so alive in all my life.

VII—Annealed

I opened the door to see the simple smile of Peter Ververken greeting me. He extended his hand.

"How are you, Andy?"

"I'm doing great. Found the feeling I like in my legs and I am excited to get back to racing."

Peter let out a little chuckle.

"You are in luck. This weekend will be a UCI race in France. A 1.12 ranking and only 145 kilometers."

"Sounds like a good race to get some results. Who will be riding?"

"All of you in the house and the four guys from Gentse Feesten. Okay, tell the rest of the guys. You all take care."

With that, Peter left and I went back to watching TV. France wasn't my favorite place to race, but the roads weren't that bad and the fans were always cheering you on, even when you're the last rider on the road. The rest of the guys were excited to hear the news. We all were impatient to get back into the action with our renewed spirit after our break from the bike.

The day of the race I woke up with a strong feeling in my legs. It took a couple of days to fully recover from the epic journey I had embarked on, but I didn't care. If it had taken me two weeks to recover it was worth the benefits that particular ride conferred. The drive down to the race was different from the previous drives. Instead of the guys from the house and the Belgian riders basically ignoring each other, there was constant joking and exaggerated tales of Gentse Feesten, with the dynamic of the team changing for the better. The drive was around two hours, and when we arrived, I immediately went looking for the bathrooms. The weather was warm and I was hydrated to the point of literal explosion. Peter directed me to the building where the officials and team directors meeting would be held and I searched out the toilets.

Inside the bathroom I relived the pressure and let out a long sigh of relief. I figured while I was there I would try to drop some weight, so I went into the stalls. The first stall I came up to had a urinal-looking toilet, so I went the next one, which had the same. I went to each of the four stalls in the bathroom and couldn't find one toilet with a seat in it. Much to my dismay I had to perform the very uncomfortable and tense squatted hang maneuver that is contrary to the whole principle of the act.

Outside as I approached the team cars, I audaciously stated, "I just figured out why the French are so uptight. There are no toilet seat covers in this country, so everyone walks around constipated because they don't want to take a crap."

The group broke out in laughter and I was complimented on my perceptive observation.

The pre-race preparations had become second nature to me by this point in the season. Packing for races induced none of the stress and worries I had experienced in the start of my European campaign. My energies were now fully focused on the race and not the external distractions of life.

Peter arrived from the team meeting as Dwergje finished giving me a pre-race massage.

"Gather round, you guys. Okay—now this is going to be a tough race, but there are no standout teams here. The course is mostly large, wide-open roads, but there is one section where you turn left and hit an eight hundred-meter cobble section. These are the large, nasty cobbles, so be careful and if you flat, try to make it to the end of the section before you stop. There are two turns in the cobble section, so be careful while making the corners. The laps are just less than eight kilometers apiece and you will be doing nineteen of them. Watch for the fight for the front before the cobblestone section and the attacks to come after, which is where the race will be made. There will also be a prime of fifty euros on each lap of the race, with the exception of the first and last. So if you are there, go for some money."

The team listened attentively to the words and we all nodded in acceptance of the plans. We decided not to name a leader for the race, and none of us knew really how we were going to be riding after our break. I was feeling particularly frisky and was excited to be racing for the first time in almost a month. The fire of my drive was fueled with a new knowledge; a knowledge that burned like grade one-twenty octane race fuel and I was ready to open the throttle full tilt.

As I was preparing my jersey and finding my race food, I heard a voice from behind me.

"Hello, Andy Bennet ... how are you?"

I looked up to see the short stature of Jean-Paul, my Belgian Super-fan. I smiled.

"Ah, Jean-Paul. I am doing great. *Hoe is het met jou?*"

"Things are good. You ride strong today?"

"Yes, I plan to ride strong today. I am feeling good."

"That is good. How has the racing been going?"

"The racing was not so good the last month. I had no improvement, but I took off some time and I feel better now."

"Well, you came to Europe to learn your trade: cycling. It's a hard life, but if you learn to cycle in Europe you can cycle anywhere. It is the top of the berg. You will know what you're made of after you leave Europe, Andy."

"I know, Jean-Paul. ... Europe has changed me, it has gotten under my skin, and I feel at home and at ease here."

"That is good, Andy. I will let you finish preparing."

"Okay, Jean-Paul, you have a great day."

I finished preparing my bike and rode off to warm up for the race. Bijorn and I traded off leading out a couple of short sprint efforts to shock the systems in preparation for the race. My heart rate was elevating steadily and retreating rapidly, good signs that I was fresh and prepared for the day's endeavor. At the start of the race, I stood near Bijorn, who explained to me what the official was saying.

The mayor of the town shot a starter's pistol and the peloton was off on the 145-kilometer venture. Starting from the middle of the field, I worked my way through the sides of the field toward the front. Today I was ten-fold more attentive than the previous attempt at racing and I navigated my way through the riders and the random assembly of objects that lined the road. I flowed with the ebb of the field and used its momentum changes to propagate myself into a top-twenty position.

Once at the front of the peloton I felt my heart rate steady, and I was ready to respond to the changing conditions of the field. I surveyed the faces of the riders to see whose eyes were shifting and which riders' bodies were displaying the preemptive signs of tensing in preparation of an attack. At the front with me were Sergei, Bijorn, and Ken. They were all looking fresh and I was going to have plenty of help to cover the race at the front.

The nervousness of the field increased as we approached the kilometer before the cobbles. Riders started to bob and weave their way through the field, fighting over every inch of position to gain an advantage. I kept a French rider at bay behind me as the field slowed down as it entered the cobbles. I kept my momentum up and shifted down to a large gear.

About a month ago, Ken told me the secret to riding cobbles was using a big gear because you don't lose as much power compared to spinning and you have a lot less chance of dropping your chain. The only problem is if you weren't feeling good, pushing the big gear would be a problem; but not today, as my power was high and I was gliding over the cobbles with ease. Exiting the cobbles, the rattling stopped and I looked down to my heart rate monitor … 170. I hadn't even exceeded lactic threshold with the effort. The three small numbers instilled me with confidence and I was ready to not only follow the attacks, but also to put in a few myself.

Right after the cobbles, the front riders kept up the pace and I followed the wheel in front of me, seeking relief from the wind. Each of my pedal stokes were solid and I helped to push the pace faster when it was my turn at the front. As I faded back, I noticed Ken and Bijorn were also in the rotation. I followed through with the rotation and waited for the right moment to come. The riders at the front started to soft-pedal, not completely but just enough to allow the speed to slow down just a little. This instant is where the "right moment" almost always comes. The point where the riders with the legs that are still fresh attack, and the riders who aren't in the mix want to relax and recover. The separation of the fodder from the leaders happens.

The first to attack was a French rider on the Crédit Agricole Division III team. He was a tall rider and the lead riders quickly latched on to his wheel. Once again, the field was stretched thin and to the point where it was a ready to snap. I waited for the Crédit Agricole rider to start to soft-pedal and I put my head down and attacked. The wind was slightly from the left, so I moved far to the right to give relief to no rider behind me. I wanted to stretch the elasticity of the field to where one rider would falter and the chain would be broken and a breakaway is formed. I put in a solid minute's worth of effort and signaled my elbow to have the next rider in line pull through.

As I faded back I looked between my right arm to see a small gap and at the front was Ken. He was pushing the pace, but not with an effort that brought intense strain to his face. He was betting on keeping a high enough pace that the riders who were behind wouldn't want to pass, but going easy enough he could sustain the effort. Three back from Ken I could see Bijorn. With those two at the front not willing to work, I was beginning to like the odds of this breakaway working.

I continued with the rotation and we pushed each other hard through the rest of the lap. I couldn't speak a foreign language, but by this point in the season I spoke fluent international cycling, which meant I could yell both words of encouragement and curses in most every major European language. It's kind of hard not to pick up the lingo when it's being yelled all the time.

We passed the finish line and shortly we saw a motorbike pass us with an old, decrepit chalkboard. Written on the board was, " '40." We were established, but there was still a long way to go in the race and I was keeping a reserved composure for the long haul. Each pull I went hard, but never beyond my means. The cobblestone section was where our group was distancing ourselves. Our small group of four was able to pick and choose the smoothest line and we were not subject to the erratic slowdowns the peloton experienced.

After seven laps of the race, I heard a honking behind me. I looked over my shoulder to see the BASE-Duvel team car behind me. I drifted back to switch out my bottles and grab some food. As I rolled back, Peter held out a bottle and I switched it out. The next one he held out, he told me to hold onto.

"Andy, you're looking good. The peloton is over a minute behind you. The guys are all over the front like stink on shit and keeping good control. Stay relaxed and steady." I nodded in acknowledgment. He looked over at me. "Okay now, hold on!"

Just then I heard the purr of the Peugeot engine roar as the bottle in my hand pulled my arm straight and I accelerated forward with the car. I pulled hard on the bottle and catapulted myself back into the breakaway and retook my place in sharing the work.

The breakaway kept going hard, and we weren't slowing down as the laps continued. Each time the sprint for a prime came up we just rotated through and shared in the wealth. No one was in a mood to challenge each other for something so small; we were all in this for the long haul. After the seventeenth lap, the motorbike once again came up to give us a split, but this time it was atypical. The board read, " '50," then "1'35."

I heard the distinct tone of the BASE-Duvel car horn behind me and I drifted back to talk with Peter and replenish my bottles. Peter gave me the lowdown.

"Andy, a group of five has broken off the front of the field. Ken is in there. So you will have some help soon."

I gave him the thumbs-up and received my water bottle launch for reentry into the breakaway.

The chase group took over a lap to catch us, and going into the cobble section, they made contact. The cobbles by this point in the race were taking their toll on me and I felt a twinge in my back start to spasm slightly. I moved my hands to the hoods and relieved the pressure, and I made it to the end of the section without inciting a full-on spasm. All I could think was how nice it was that I only had one more time across the evil span of road known as cobbles.

The smooth road eased the pace, and Ken rolled up next to me.

"Hey, mate. How ya doin'?"

"I'm hurting, but here. You?"

"The chase to the front was hard, but I still got a couple more matches left to burn on the last lap."

"Good, 'cause I'm down to rubbing two sticks together to get the fire going!"

I rolled into the protection of the largest rider in the breakaway and started to take half pulls when I was at the front. I wanted to be ready for the finishing lap and save my last bit of reserves.

On the finishing straight, the crowd was intense and thick, at least three deep in the last two hundred meters. The long straight shot to the line gave the advantage to a strong team with a group of guys who could perform a well-planned lead-out, but today's race winner would have to wield precise timing in a small-group sprint. Pick an attack too early and you won't make the distance; too late and you won't have enough road.

The announcer started into a fury of words all running together, as he never seemed to pause to catch his breath. The makeup of the breakaway was favorable for the masses, with only Ken and me along with Crédit Agricole having teammates. I could quickly see this turning into a free-for-all, with attacks coming from every direction quickly. The pace was steady and strong after the finish, but as we approached the cobblestone section, everyone started to look at one another. The chess match began.

Ken was at the front of the group and I positioned myself in the middle of the break. As the rattle of the water bottles signaled our entry into the cobbles, the pace slowly increased and the power requirement was reaching my threshold limit for sustaining the effort. As the first rider made the first corner in the cobbles, I heard the distinctive bang of a tire flatting. I made the next corner hoping I wasn't the one fated to flat after my long effort. I watched the rider in front me slow down and then start to slide as his rear tire separated from the rim. I hit the brakes, narrowly navigating my way around him as he started sliding on the cobbles.

My momentum was slowed and I started to mash against the pedals, but then I noticed the gap. The front three riders, including Ken, were a few meters ahead. I saw this chance and bet on my Kiwi friend. I kept rolling, but didn't increase my speed, just kept the steady tempo going as the gap grew larger with each second. It took about half a minute for the riders behind me to figure out what had just happened, as the attention span while cycling at your threshold zone is rather short.

The situation was four riders behind and three ahead, separated by less than fifty meters. The lead riders noted the advantage, and I saw Ken move quickly to the front to drill the pace. The other riders with me were yelling a long list of obscenities, in several languages. Most of the English ones were close to correct, but just a bit off. I looked at the jerseys up the road and then at those in my group and noticed the other Crédit Agricole had made the split, narrowing the pursuit down to three against two. I liked those odds.

The other two riders attacked in vain, but the Crédit Agricole rider and I attached ourselves to their wheels like dirt on a chain. I could see the lead riders on the horizon, but it was hard to distinguish who was where and how far ahead lay the finish line—only a small blur in the distance ahead. I watched the faces of the other riders for signals and signs of weakness or attack. The approach to the finish line was a brief game of cat and mouse. I held my second position firmly but let the Crédit Agricole rider get the jump on me, and I ran out of road to catch him by the finish line but I still threw my bike in a fleeting aspiration that I could span the intangible distance. I soft-pedaled to the side of the road, dismounted my bike, and lay on the ground. I didn't even know if I had the energy to breathe.

As I stared up into the sky, I saw the gleaming smile of Ken come into view.

I muttered out, "So what is it?"

He said nothing, raising slowly a solitary finger toward the sky.

"You're shittin' me!!!"

"Mate, you know I don't shite around. Thanks for the help."

Ken extended a hand down and I raised mine in acceptance as he pulled me to my feet. I couldn't believe the team had just won a race! I wanted to go take on another twenty laps of that course. The feeling of victory is an energy restorer of unlimited bounds.

The victory ceremony was really cool, as Ken had to pose for several different photos with an array of sponsors. He was most pleased when the beauty queen of the province gave him his victory bouquet and a kiss on each cheek. I could have sworn I saw Ken blush, but it could have been the dehydration flushing his cheeks.

While I watched Ken stumble through, trying to answer questions in French, I heard a familiar voice behind me say, "Congratulations, Andy Bennet. You are learning your job well."

It was Jean-Paul.

"Thanks ... that was a damn hard race!"

"Yes, and you did very well. Good luck in the coming months."

With that he shook my hand goodbye and I returned my attention to the awards ceremony.

After the race, Peter gathered the riders together.

"Guys, that is what I call racing! You ride that smart every race and we will have more flowers than a florist. Oh yeah, and this. ..." Peter pulled out a bundle of envelopes from his folder. "Today we took the win, fifth, and twelfth along with the team overall. We made some good money today!"

Ken then broke in, "I do have to say I couldn't have done this without Andy. Because of his effort at the front, I didn't have to work in the breakaway. I had the energy to make the right move. Thanks, Andy."

I looked over at him and nodded.

"No problem. Any time."

* * *

I gazed through the glass pressed against my forehead as the road moved in a blur of gray contrasting with the green background of the land. The past month went by in a flash of reality that came so quickly I felt as if I was stuck in the midst of a dream. The momentum of the win in France propelled the team forward, racking up one more UCI win and three Kermesse victories. In fact, I had placed in the top three just last week in Beernem at a large Kermesse. The bookies now placed my odds in the single digits, a good sign I was a rider of concern.

The BASE-Duvel team was being invited to more races than it could handle, but today's race we made room for a UCI 1.6 and a *Topcompetitie* race, the select paragon of ten races for an overall competition in Belgium. These races are the highest level of amateur racing in Belgium, and with only a few points separating the leaders, the top riders were out for blood, with today's race being the second to last in the series. Ken's procuring of a start list from Peter didn't help in my mental preparation.

He ran down the list of teams and names ... Quick-Step DIII, Crédit Agricole DIII, ABX-Go Pass, Rabobank DIII, and a host of national teams. He started sounding off names and the respective Division I and -II teams each rider had signed contracts with for the next year. It was glaringly obvious this wasn't going to be a lowly 1.12 in France. It was the big show and I needed to bring in my mental game as well as my physical game. The one thing I liked about going into the race, even with the team's recent success, was that we were just pack fodder in the minds of the other riders.

It's a dangerous thing to place a limit on something, because when that limit is exceeded, more often than not it's to your detriment. The team had the advantage of no expectations and no pressure.

As Peter stated it, "Earlier this year, I wouldn't have thought of us going to this race; now we are here. It's a chance, guys, a chance to show your true colors, how deep your drive goes, and how much that inner fire fuels you. Leave them speechless."

My inner dialogue was suspended as the roadway before me focused into a crystal clear image: the car had stopped. The race started in Antwerp, so the drive was relatively short and we had plenty of downtime to get ready at our leisure. I walked around a little bit to loosen up the legs as well as my nerves. I hadn't remembered being this tense in a long time, not since my first Kermesse race all the way back in March. It seemed like an eternity to go.

I walked back to the team cars and I sat down in a chair next to Sergei.

I guess he sensed my tension as he started off freestyling, "One thing I know is that life is short—So listen up homeboy, give this a thought—The next time someone's teaching why don't you get taught?"

Despite its idiotic nature, the act pulled away a good bit of the stress from me. He knew me quite well by this point in the season, as did everyone in the house. We knew the small nuances of a teammate's quirks, and cohesiveness naturally came about from this knowledge.

My nerves began to settle as I went through my ritualistic pre-race preparations. The familiarity of the actions rested the mind and brought about the awakening of the body to prepare for the assault on the very fibers of being that held it together. I pinned my number on in precise fashion and held it up in front of me. It read "Het Nieuwsblad" for the Flemish newspaper that sponsored the Topcompetitie race series. I released a deep, long breath and exhaled the last of my worries.

Peter called all of us together for our pre-race meeting. I could see the seriousness in the gleam of his eyes and the precise movements of his body. His tone began in the firm directness of a drill sergeant.

"Guys, I will not lie to you. No one thought our team would be here today, not this season, but here we are. We are here because we are good enough. Let the other teams look at us and laugh. It gives us the advantage: no pressure. Our sponsors are happy enough to have us in the race. Those other teams, they are the ones with the pressure: the sponsors who are breathing down their necks for wins. All we have to do is ride our bikes, race till we feel we can't race any harder, then dig in and push it farther. Now, for the race … it's long at 190 kilometers, but the roads are flat around here, so look for a race just over four hours. There will be two loops; the first is ninety kilometers and the second is fifty kilometers. Then you will have ten laps of five kilometers for the finishing circuit. If a breakaway makes the finishing circuit with a lead over a minute, you will have trouble catching it because of slowdowns caused by the turns. The team has drawn fourth position in the caravan, a very good break for us. As far as tactics, we have several riders all capable of winning, so talk to each other, and if you see a chance, take it. That's all I got to say. … Go ride your limits and then some."

The speech left most of us a bit taken aback. I hadn't seen this stern side of Peter before, but it came with an air of assurance that collectively calmed the group and instilled us all with confidence. We were ready for deployment into the war zone of the peloton. Dwergje waddled around and handed out all the bottles and made sure we all got a little extra bit of care in our warm-up massage. I watched him take immense care in his already intensive preparations of the race food and bottles.

I started off on a leisurely roll down the road to loosen the legs and put in a few efforts for my pre-race system shock. The air whisked my cheeks as I felt the consistent thump of the expansion joints of the concrete under my tires. The mild temperatures of Belgian summers and the flawless blue of the clear sky made for pleasurable and very favorable race conditions.

My pre-race efforts went by with little problem. I felt good, but I couldn't quite tell if I felt great. I was never able to tell that fact until I got in the race and let the nerves settle down and my heart rate level off to my zone of comfort. I watched the other riders ride past me.

Only one of us would win. One rider in a field of nearly two hundred. Other sports had the luxury of teammates, time-outs, and rest. Cycling was so individual; even with a world-class team around a rider, it was still up to that rider to push the pedals. He has no one to rely on but himself and no collective effort by a team could help. I liked the individuality of the sport. It was you who determined your fate; your effort into cycling was what you got out.

I rolled over to the starting area to study the finish line. The organization picked a long road with an ever-so-slight rise to the finish. It was so subtle that most people wouldn't realize it, but it was there. The impact on the race wasn't much, but it was one of the many factors to think about for the sprint. I looked at the road surface, the wind direction, and it was all a draw; there wasn't going to be much way to advantage yourself in the sprint. Pure power and timing would be the needed ingredients in a sprint win, if it came down to one. I glanced at my watch: 10:50, time to head to the starting area for the beginning of the race.

I pushed and edged as far to the front of the line as I could get. I wanted to have as much advantage as I could in the race and didn't want to expend any extra energy gaining ground and working my way to the front. I looked behind me and there were so many riders filling the wide road. There was going to be a lot of horsepower in the field today and it would be some fast pace setting.

I found Ken to right and he smiled.

"Andy, you ready for this?"

"Ready ... uh ..."

The question was a trigger pulled; it released a spark in my brain, igniting the realization of all that I had done, how far I was, and the distance I had traveled to this very moment. If there was a moment I wanted to come to during my European season, this was the moment. Ready? I was more than ready.

"Yeah, I am pleasantly prepared."

"Goodonya, mate. That's the spirit."

I watched the lead official start his speech, and my breaths became shorter in interval. He finished up his speech and entered the lead vehicle. He popped out of the sunroof of the lead vehicle, raised a red flag, and the vehicle accelerated off. The race rolled off and I kept my position at the front while we wandered our way through the first two kilometers of neutral rollout. As we hit the main road, the red flag came down and the green flag was waved; the deployment into the war zone began.

The attacks were serious, intense, and without mercy. I did all the hiding I could in the field, burying myself deep within the belly of the beast. I wanted to let the riders of the larger teams handle the attacks while I conserved my energies for the right moment when I could advantage them into a good return. The eclectic elements that made up a race can never be quantified, so a keen instinct is always necessary. The sheer number of riders combined with the fast, flat course meant a small breakaway was unlikely to survive and a small group would be the winners.

The riders at the front pushed the pace fast; so fast, in fact, I thought a rider would be insane to try to break free. But insanity was in abundance as a number of riders tried in vain to attack on the opposite side of the peloton's front to gain a small advantage, only to be reeled back. The larger teams continued to control and dominate the race throughout the first fifty kilometers, each trading off attacks and being chased down. The façade of the control of an uncontrollable element like a race was eventually broken when a small group of five riders made their way off the front after seventy-five kilometers in the race.

These riders were nothing more than a control element. The riders at the front let the advantage roll up to two minutes then continued to push the steady pace. With the riders up the road the mentality of the peloton turned from proactive to reactive, wherein riders don't want to attack but chase down the break. The day would be long for the riders pushing the front.

The peloton crossed the finish line after the ninety-kilometer loop, and I was in a good zone. I hadn't had to push my body to its limits yet and the steady pace was bearable. The field started to pick up the pace at the 120-kilometer mark of the race. The lead riders wanted to fold the hand being played, reshuffle the deck, and deal a new hand to be played. I was keeping myself buried in the middle of the field as we turned onto a large road, one of the N-class highways in Belgium that are similar to farm-to-market roads in the U.S.

It was then that the one thing every cyclist fears and which is an evitable part of the uncontrollable nature of the race, happened: a flat started its evil hiss from my rear wheel. The air quickly escaped and left me unsteady upon my bike, with little control over my rear wheel. I rode the wheel through the rear of the peloton and raised my right hand at the back of the field. I made my way to the right-hand side and kept riding till I heard the distinctive horn of the BASE-Duvel team car.

I dismounted cyclocross-style and unlatched my rear wheel. I was releasing my rear wheel when Dwergje was there with a wheel in hand. He mounted the wheel in precise precision, changed both my bottles, and had me on my bike in less than ten seconds. As I preformed my running remount, I felt Dwergje's small hands give me a push of five men. I heard the squeal of tires behind me as Peter rally-styled his way beside me.

We spent the next ten minutes steadily working our way through the caravan and to the rear of the peloton. As we approached the commissioner's car, it was the end of the line for the BASE-Duvel express. I came around the left-hand side of the car to see a small water bottle being held out. I approached the water bottle, grabbed hold, and Peter accelerated as I was propelled into the field. I watched the commissioner pop out of the sunroof of his car and glance scoldingly back at Peter, who pulled up his shoulders and gave the "'what did I do?" innocent look of a five-year-old caught with his hand in the cookie jar.

I worked my way through the field, and toward the front I saw Sergei and Bijorn. Bijorn saw me.

"Good of you to join us, Andy. Flats suck."

"Tell me about it."

"The front break was reeled in and there is another group of about twelve riders up the road. I think that was the winning move."

I felt my breathing pause momentarily in disbelief. No wonder the chase back on the caravan was so hard: the peloton was going full tilt, and now the race is up the road and I am stuck in the field.

"Damn it, we got anyone up there?"

"Not that I know of ... no, don't think so."

Devastation was more than feeling; it was the reality of the situation. I didn't know what to do, but I wanted to go for a win, not some lowly placing in the teens no one would care about in two days. I looked over at Bijorn.

"We have to chase down that break!"

"Are you crazy, Andy? We have good riders, but that is *the* break."

As I tried to plead my case to Bijorn I saw two of the Quick-Step DIII riders pass me on the left, then another two. It was as if they were drawn to the front by some unknown magnetic force.

I paused from my persuasion and thought for a second. I looked over to Bijorn.

"Did Quick-Step make the break?"

"Uh, maybe ..."

129

"Then why are they all going to the front?"

I saw the composition of the race change from bad to manageable in one heartbeat. I had an ally through a common enemy: the break. I moved my way to the front of the race and positioned myself a few riders behind the forming line of blue and silver.

In less than a minute, there was a full squadron of eight Quick-Step riders at the front and they began to turn up the pace in pursuit of the breakaway. The blue train steamed ahead and started to string out the field into a slim line of riders holding dear to the safe protection of the wheel in front of them. At the finish line I heard the announcer in several languages tell the time gap to be one minute and ten seconds. Fifty kilometers of racing was a long way, but through winding streets it was going to be a hard chase to reel back.

The first three laps of the finishing circuit, the Quick-Step team steamed forward without making a single second of advantage on the breakaway. Each time around it was the same time gap. The next three laps saw the field's rear riders start to lag and fall off from the consistent acceleration of the tail end, while the gap to the leaders was brought down to forty-five seconds. The next lap, the break was ten seconds less. By three laps to go, the gap was in the twenties. And with two laps to go, we could see the break in sight on longer straights. With one lap to go, we were ten seconds off from the riders.

I looked ahead and my animal instincts took over as I saw the riders in the break. I watched attentively at the actions and reactions of the riders around me, as the reshuffle of the peloton was going to be tricky. The peloton charged as the Quick-Step team started its final push for the front break, and when the field was within striking distance the attacks came. Riders who were waiting to bridge the gap went, and I followed the wheels in front of me. The intense convergence of the two groups caused a momentary lapse of logical procedure, and I took full advantage, following a rider who was trucking full steam ahead through the randomness of the chaos.

I gritted my teeth, pulled my arms taut, and dug deep just to keep the wheel of the rider in front of me. I glanced down at my computer: fifty-eight kilometers per hour. We were almost at full-sprint speed. I focused intensely and separated my mind from reason to allow my body to delve into realms of intense displeasure. I felt the pains of lactic acid coursing through my veins but I ignored the bodily pleas for ceasing.

The rider signaled me to take my turn, and I pushed the pace even harder as we made the turns through the outskirts of Antwerp. I turned my attention outward and focused on the narrow scope of reality my eyes displayed. Details and time were blended into a tapestry of distorted reality as I coped with the pain. I was in the zone.

I finished my pull and as I drifted back, I stood up to accelerate onto the wheel of the rider while glancing back to see the field a fair distance behind. The gap was established. I took temporary relief behind the rider as we sped our way around the corners strewn throughout in the final kilometers of the race. I kept the pace high and we drove each other harder and harder with each pull.

The gap was enough that on the last two pulls through I couldn't see any riders behind. The roads were short, so there was an unknown beast behind, waiting to attack. I gritted my teeth some more and pushed the fear out of me with each pedal stroke. We made the final left-hand corner, and meters later passed under the red flag suspended from a large, white, inflated, sponsor display. The final kilometer.

I took my pull to the front and continued to go as hard I as could. I went to pull off to force the rider to take the lead for the final sprint, but he would not pass. I yelled at him to take his pull, but he stayed on my rear wheel. I moved all the way to the right-hand side of the road and looked back to see the presence of the peloton on the horizon. The risk was too great to play a slow chess match with the rider, so I accelerated to a reasonable speed and held my ground on the right while watching the rider intensely.

At seven hundred meters, the rider was still there. At five hundred meters, I picked up the pace a bit more when I saw him tighten his grip on his bars. At four hundred meters, I stood up to accelerate the pace. At three hundred, he started to make his move around. At two hundred, I had already matched his speed and was pulling ahead. At one hundred meters, he was faltering, and finally at fifty meters, my advantage was over a wheel. At the finish, my hands punched celebratory in the air. I won the race.

I rolled across the line, hands wide apart, with a large smile on my face. The feeling of victory ran from the tips of my fingers, down my arms, across my spine, down my legs, and to the tips of my toes. It was a long time since I had felt the distinctive pleasure of winning, and it had never tasted as sweet as it did that very moment. My long journey in

Europe was filled with strife and problems, but a single moment brought it all into perspective.

I rolled over to the side of the road and was immediately surrounded by crowds of people all sputtering out phrases in Flemish I couldn't even understand. Through the crowd I saw Ken, Sergei, and Troy pushing their way over to me. I muscled my way over to them and we all grabbed each other and started jumping up and down. Ken was yelling,

"You did it, Andy, it was amazing!"

"I know—it's so surreal!"

A man worked his way over to me and put his hand on my shoulder.

"Come with me, we need to do awards soon."

I walked over with him to behind the awards stage, where I found Peter waiting for me with Dwergje. Peter had a large grin on his face and handed me a waterbottle.

"You're tough as nails, Andy, tough as nails."

I grinned and took a clean washcloth from Dwergje to clean up. He gave me a clean, long-sleeved jersey to wear. The man from the crowd came to me.

"It is time, Andy Bennet."

I walked from the backside of the stage to the front and ascended the stairs. As I walked up each step, I looked at the surreal surroundings around me. Each face in the crowd stared at me, the victor of the race. I couldn't help but pull my cheeks wide and almost giggled at the excitement at it all. Onstage the announcer came up and introduced me to everyone. A beautiful podium girl came over with a bouquet of flowers and a kiss then another girl came over with a trophy. I raised the awards in the air in glorious fashion. I looked up at the flowers raised high in my right hand and then thought of Jurgen … I was going to have to send these flowers in the mail to him; he'd get a kick out of that.

The announcer came over to me and asked me a few questions about where I was from and why I came to Belgium to race. Then he asked me a final question:

"What are your plans for the future?"

In a flash, the reality of my European experience hit me. I had just traveled to Europe, raced my heart out, and accomplished everything I had planned. I went through the meat grinder of European racing and it hadn't chewed me up. In fact, Belgium had chiseled me in into a fine and strong racer. I felt the wealth of opportunity and potential that lay before me, and it sent chills coursing through my spine.

I looked over to the announcer.

"I know not what the future brings; only what I can bring to the future."

About The Author

Cobblestone Dreams is Brent Bender's first major venture into the realm of novel-writing, but he has been an avid writer most of his life. Taking his passion for the bike and writing, he presents the inner workings of cycling in words. Brent enjoys bicycle racing, riding, and the thrills of driving his body beyond its known limits.

Printed in the United States
96811LV00003B/225/A

9 781418 494872